# JAY-JAY and the PEKING MONSTER

# JAY-JAY and the PEKING MONSTER

## HAL G. EVARTS

CHARLES SCRIBNER'S SONS • NEW YORK

Copyright © 1978 Hal G. Evarts

Library of Congress Cataloging in Publication Data

Evarts, Hal George, 1915–
  Jay-Jay and the Peking monster.

  SUMMARY: A Southern California boy finds a box of
bones that may be the remains of prehistoric Peking
Man which have been missing from a museum since
World War II.
  [1. Peking man—Fiction.  2. Science fiction]
I. Title.
PZ7.E895Jay      [Fic]      77-27426
ISBN 0-684-15547-8

1 3 5 7 9 11 13 15 17 19 V/C 20 18 16 14 12 10 8 6 4 2

Printed in the United States of America

*For*
*John and Margie,*
*my favorite co-cultivators*

# JAY-JAY and the PEKING MONSTER

# ONE

JAY-JAY DOWSER HAD been watching the weather anxiously all day. Late that afternoon a low-hanging inversion layer, a gray-brown smudge of fog and smog, drifted inland from the Pacific. Probably it would hug the valleys and the foot-hills until burned off by the sun next morning, an outlook which freed Jay-jay from one concern. A clear, bright, moonlit night he needed like a case of mumps.

Of course, he told himself, he didn't *have* to go through with this. He could change his mind and fake some excuse. He could say he'd suddenly taken sick. Or that the truck had broken down. Nobody could blame him. So why not? Because he needed the money, that's why.

Don't chicken out now, Dowser.

At six o'clock he turned on his transistor and listened to the news, a dreary chronicle of riot, revolution, murder, and assorted mayhem. The weather forecast, which came last, confirmed his own prediction: evening and early morning overcast, clearing before noon, fairly typical for coastal southern California. Plus possible thunder storms over the mountains late tomorrow.

Jay-jay digested this morsel of information and climbed down the ladder from his room in the water tower to look for his aunt. When the telephone began to ring inside the house he gave a guilty start and broke into a trot. He suspected who the caller would be—on this day at this hour almost had to be. The voice of his conscience.

"Hello, kiddo," a gravel voice said when Jay-jay picked up the receiver. "It's me."

"Me" was Master Sergeant Moose Majeski, United States Marine Corps, grizzled combat veteran of three wars on land and sea, now holding down a desk job on the nearby training base of Camp Pennington. "Hi, Moose," Jay-jay said uneasily. "I guessed it was you."

"Did, huh?" Moose rumbled. "You all set for tonight?"

"Yes, but I've been thinking—"

"Didja check out the rendezvous point?"

"This morning. It's okay, but—"

"Bring plenty of eats. And I mean *plenty*. I know what it's like. I ran that course myself once."

"Moose, listen, I can't—"

"Kid?" There was an ominous pause. "You're not getting cold feet, are you?"

Jay-jay swallowed. Without closing his eyes he could picture Sergeant Majeski's barrel chest, size 17 neck, bulldog jaw. "Who, me? The thing is—"

"You want that dough or not?" Moose demanded.

"Sure I do," Jay-jay said, "Only—"

"Then be there. Twenty-four hundred hours. Sharp. You let my buddies down I'll take it personal. Understand?"

"Yes, sir. Gotcha!"

"Good. And kiddo—" Moose gave a raspy little chuckle that alarmed Jay-jay more than any threat, "watch yourself. Don't get caught or the deal's off."

"Caught? Hey, Moose, what—"

The sergeant chuckled again and hung up.

Jay-jay was surprised to find his hand trembling. Why, oh why, had he gotten mixed up in this screwball scheme—Operation Survival, Moose called it—in the first place? Too late for second thoughts or alibis. No way to pass the buck, he told himself. You bought the whole package, chum, and now you gotta deliver. Or else.

Stepping outside, he glanced at the peeling weathered sign which informed the world:

LAS PULGAS FARM

ORGANIC FRUITS AND VEGETABLES

EXOTIC PLANTS

H. GRIBBEN, PROP.

*Las Pulgas* means "The Fleas," so named by Spanish explorers who, some two centuries earlier, had camped alongside the nearby creek one night and found their blankets jumping with those tiny insects. Four acres of boulders, native brush, and ancient oak trees, one acre of cultivation. The Flea Farm had been Jay-jay's home for the past ten years, ever since his parents died in a plane crash, long enough for him to outgrow his childish embarrassment at the name.

So far as he knew, it had never embarrassed his great-aunt Hattie Gribben, referred to by some of her snooty neighbors as "Batty Hattie."

"Hattie!" he called. "Aunt Hattie!"

She emerged from the tool shed with a hoe, clad in

/ 5

overalls, calf-high galoshes, and a raggedy, cone-shaped straw hat that gave her the appearance of a playful witch. At age seventy-odd Hattie Gribben still had her original teeth, twenty-twenty vision, and the stamina of a dray horse, although she stood only four feet eleven inches. Her splendid health she attributed to proper nutrition, a subject on which she held strong views.

"Jay-jay," she said tartly, "you needn't shout. I'm not deaf."

"Sorry," he said, "but I have to go out tonight. A delivery. Don't wait up."

"When do I ever?" Hattie's brow crinkled. "But a delivery? At night?"

"Rush order. Special customer." Hattie was no law-and-order purist but Jay-jay suspected she might not approve of his upcoming caper. Which made two of them. But necessity was the mother of something or other.

"Heavens to Betsy," she said. "Can't he wait till tomorrow?"

"He's paying a bonus," Jay-jay said. "Cash."

"Umm," she murmured. "We do have a few pesky bills."

Amen, he thought. Unpaid bills? Yes indeedy. Not to mention taxes. In their joint division of labor Hattie masterminded the production end, while Jay-jay handled long-range sales and finance. At the moment the Flea Farm bank account had a grand total of forty-seven dollars and thirty-one cents.

"Before you go," she said, "will you bring me some compost? One load should do."

"Sure. Are you getting ready to plant again?"

"Tomorrow," Hattie declared. "The signs are auspicious."

Jay-jay grinned. Hattie, a Pisces, pinned her faith on the stars and her daily horoscope. "Weather Bureau says we may get thunder storms tomorrow."

"Weather Bureau, pooh!" She sniffed. "What do those ninnies know?"

"Just passing the word along," he said and got the wheelbarrow from the shed. At the compost pit he peeled back the cover and scooped up several shovelfuls of moist black muck, a moldering residue of garbage, table scraps, and random cuttings alive with writhing grubs. This he wheeled to the far end of the garden to his aunt's experimental plot next to the fertilizer tank.

The tank, an old one-hundred-gallon wooden vat once used for wine fermentation, stood on concrete blocks above the ground and had a spigot at the bottom. It already contained fresh chicken and horse manure, two barrow loads of leaf mold, and various other substances which Jay-jay could only guess at. Into this mixture he shoveled the compost, leaned close, and took a whiff. "Smells ripe," he said. "Rarin' to go."

"Not quite." From some pouch in her overalls Hattie produced a pint-sized bottle of a scummy greenish liquid, unscrewed the cap, and poured the contents into the vat.

"What's that?"

"Ask me no questions and I'll tell you no lies," Hattie said airily. "It's potent, though."

Jay-jay shook his head in wonder. When mixing her batches of fertilizer Hattie, like a master chef, followed no formula or recipe, measured out the ingredients by hunch and whim, by guess and by gosh. Her secrets she kept to herself. "Well, good luck this time," he said.

"I don't trust in luck." She tapped a finger against her head. "Only in what's up here."

"I don't either," he said, "but I could use a little tonight. Let's go eat."

After supper, when Hattie retired to study her astrological charts, Jay-jay gathered another dozen fresh eggs from the henhouse and put them on the stove to boil. Then he set about assembling his wares: ten loaves of whole-grain bread he'd baked the day before, some avocados he'd picked last week and left to ripen, some oranges and tomatoes, and a bag of Hattie's dietetic cookies.

From the garden he pulled up several heads of lettuce and clumps of carrots and for good measure threw in a few onions. About the zucchini he debated, then decided that his customers, however hungry, might not much care for raw squash as a midnight snack. By the time he'd washed the vegetables, his eggs had cooled. All these items he divided into two equal piles and stuffed into gunny sacks, which he tied securely at the top with cord and lugged out to the pickup.

The sacks weighed about twenty pounds apiece, Jay-jay estimated, which averaged out to four pounds per man. Not exactly a feast, but enough to ward off starvation.

Night had fallen and out in the chaparral a cricket chorus was tuning up. Jay-jay glanced at the murky sky for reassurance, then at his watch. Lots of time yet but already the butterflies were aflutter in his stomach.

Returning to the house, Jay-jay tiptoed into Hattie's room and found her asleep. He kissed her on the cheek, switched off the light, and tiptoed out again. For better or for worse, Operation Survival was under way. But whose survival? Jay-jay wondered. Mine? Or the Marines?

The Ford's odometer registered five thousand miles but during its checkered career, he knew, the venerable truck had logged at least two hundred thousand more. The engine coughed and sputtered but caught on the first try. Jay-jay eased out to the county road and turned right, crossing the narrow bridge over Las Pulgas Creek, which ran dry eleven months of the year.

At the first mailbox, lettered ZINK, he slowed and braked to a stop. To put it charitably, the Zink place, which bordered Hattie's property to the south, looked seedy and rundown, in need of tender loving care. The only crop raised by Walter Zink, who called himself a "gentleman rancher," seemed to be weeds. For a living the man wrote science fiction novels. A single light burned in the front room of the house and the staccato rhythm of a typewriter drifted out on the evening air.

After due deliberation Jay-jay flicked his headlights off and on three times. Frankly, he admitted, he didn't savor the prospect of waiting alone in the dark. Also, in case he did get caught (that couldn't happen, naturally) he might need a backup partner to raise the alarm and bail him out. If *bail* was the word.

Almost at once the front door opened and a slender figure in jeans and T-shirt appeared. When she made out the truck, Carla Zink flipped a salute and sauntered over to the road. "Hi, Dowser," she said. "Thanks for ringing the doorbell."

"Me and my bad manners," he said. Carla, a tall leggy sixteen, was no sweet, demure girl-next-door type. She had a straight-A brain, a cannonball tennis serve, and a jaw as square as Moose Majeski's. "I didn't want to disturb your father. Does he always work this late?"

"When Daddy gets going on a new book he writes nonstop," she said. "You out cruising tonight?"

"Moonlighting. How'd you like to earn five bucks?"

"Doing what?"

"Nothing much. Watch my truck a few minutes while I run an errand."

Carla gave him a long quizzical stare. "The price is right," she said, "but it sounds too simple. What's the catch?"

"No catch," he told her. "I'll have you back home and beddy-bye a little after twelve."

"Dowser, you've got a shifty look. I think you're conning me. Would this errand be maybe lowdown and sneaky? Illegal?"

"Ten bucks," Jay-jay offered. "I'll explain when we get there."

Carla sighed. "Anything to help a friend in need. Wait a sec." She hurried back to the house, reemerged a minute later with a jacket draped over her shoulders, closed the door, and locked it. The typewriter chattered on without a break.

When she slid into the cab beside him Jay-jay said, "How come you didn't tell your father? Won't he worry?"

"Worry?" Carla said. "Daddy concentrates so hard he wouldn't notice a typhoon."

So be it, Jay-jay thought. The Zinks had moved here from San Diego a few months earlier "to beat the rat race," as Carla put it. Jay-jay had not seen much of Daddy, and of Mother Zink he had yet to see a trace.

They seemed to be a clannish family. But maybe all sci-fi writers were a little peculiar.

He nosed the truck around and drove back to the bridge, where he made a sharp turn, and eased onto a dim set of wheel tracks that wound along the creek bank. Giant oaks formed a leafy tunnel overhead and brush pressed close on either side. Now and then the headlights picked out the pale trunk of a sycamore. The track grew rapidly worse, rutted and rocky and partially overgrown. Jay-jay crept along in low gear with his right foot riding the brake pedal.

"Hey!" Carla cried. "This is a dead end. Where—"

"Patience, woman," Jay-jay muttered. "Not much farther."

Some two miles below the bridge the trail ended at a clearing. Jay-jay parked behind a clump of toyon, killed the lights and motor. In the deep night silence a frog croaked down in the creek bottom. The end-of-summer smell of dust and sage was overpowering. "Now you know where we are?" he asked.

"Sure I know," Carla said. "And I don't like it."

"I promised to meet some guys tonight," he said. "Marines."

"Who else would you meet here?" she said. "Little pointy-headed people from Mars? But why?"

"It's sort of far out. Every month the brass at Pennington run what they call a Physical Fitness Field Training Exercise. Turn a bunch of noncoms loose in the boondocks for five days to sweat off the flab."

"What are noncoms?"

"Noncommissioned officers. The ones with stripes on

their sleeves. Corporals and sergeants. They get a canteen of water apiece, pocket knife, pack of matches, some cord for making snares. That's it. Idea is to live off the land."

"For five whole days? What do they use for food?"

"They catch their own," Jay-jay said. "Dig up their own. Whatever they can scrounge. Real tough Leather-necks."

"Ugh! You mean, like snakes and bugs? That's awful! They must be half-dead." Carla paused, her profile silhouetted against the open window, her breathing suddenly faster. "Now the light dawns. You rat, Dowser! Are you preying on those poor famished boys?"

"Boys?" Jay-jay laughed. "You should meet Moose Majeski, the boy who dreamed this up. To win a bet from his buddies."

"That's not funny. It's disgusting! Aren't you ashamed?"

"Nope, but I'm kind of nervous." Jay-jay climbed out of the cab and peered across the barren, naked land that tilted downward into blackness. "You wait here till I get back."

"Oh, sure." Carla tossed her hair. "Great big macho trip. What if somebody comes along?"

"Can you whistle?"

She put two fingers between her teeth and gave a shrill ear-piercing blast.

"Roger," Jay-jay said. "This shouldn't take long."

He tucked a flashlight in his hip pocket, lifted the two sacks from the truck bed, and slung one over each shoulder. Burdened like a pack mule, he advanced cautiously across open ground some hundred yards until he reached the fence. The fence, eight feet of chain link steel topped by a three-strand vee of wicked-looking barbed wire, stretched away in either direction toward infinity. It supported a large metal sign:

UNITED STATES MARINE CORPS

DANGER   KEEP OUT

Jay-jay set down his merchandise, noting that the fence served equally well to keep Marines *in*. He glanced right and left, then straight ahead through the chain link diamond mesh. Nothing. No sound, no movement, zero. Once again he checked his watch. He'd timed this close. Maybe too close.

Suppose, he thought, they've come and gone; for some reason they couldn't wait. Suppose they don't show at all. Maybe *they've* chickened out. But Marines don't chicken. He peered back at the barely visible toyon clump and the invisible truck, wondering how Carla felt. Suppose Daddy *did* look up from his typewriter, began to worry, and called the cops.

Dowser, cool it. You're too young for an ulcer.

The howl of a coyote not far away raised the hairs on the nape of his neck. Beyond the fence he could now distinguish the black serpentine course of Las Pulgas Creek. This remote backside of Camp P, so rumors went, abounded with wildlife—foxes, mountain lions, deer. Maybe his customers had hunted down a buck and right this minute were carving up venison steaks.

A pebble rattled somewhere over there. Jay-jay swung back to his left. Out of the night a burly faceless shape in fatigues and billed cap limped into view. Behind him straggled eight or nine more, all droopy and bedraggled.

But when Jay-jay flashed his light and stepped forward they rushed the fence like a pack of ravening wolves.

In a foghorn whisper the leader said, "You the kid named Jo-jo?"

Even at close range Jay-jay could see only a pair of glittering eyes and a lot of five-o'clock shadow. He shivered at the ferocity of that stare and whispered back, "Jay-jay. Are you Murphy?"

"Yours truly. Where's the chow?"

Jay-jay indicated the two bulging sacks at his feet.

"Jay-jay," Murphy said, "how do you figure to get that stuff across to our side? Shove it through them eensy holes one hunk at a crack?"

"I guess I didn't figure."

A growl seemed to issue from ten throats in unison. "We ain't got much time," Murphy said. "You seen any MPs go by?"

"MPs?"

"Military Police. They fly perimeter patrol along the fence. In choppers."

Jay-jay shook his head. *Don't get caught or the deal's off,* Moose had warned. So now he knew the enemy by name. MPs.

"Hurry up, man," a new voice said. "I can eat a horse whole. Hair, hide, and hoofs."

"Stow it, stupid, or I'll bust your effing head," Murphy snarled. "Jay-jay, you better heave them sacks over the top. I don't see no other way."

Heave them over? Jay-jay thought. Over ten feet of fence and wire? Twenty pounds of Aunt Hattie's cookies, soft ripe avocadoes, all those tomatoes? What a mess! "Sir," he said, "maybe we can—"

"Do it! Do it now! That's an order."

"Yes, sir!" Jay-jay hefted the nearest sack with both hands and backed off a few paces. Twenty pounds? It felt like fifty. Shutting his eyes, breathing a brief prayer, he projected himself into a double spin, like a hammer thrower, and let fly. The sack sailed over the fence, clearing by several feet, and landed on the far side with a squishy thud.

"Attaboy," Murphy said. "Once more and we're in business."

Jay-jay braced himself for a repeat performance, went into his twirl, but the second time around his foot skidded at the crucial moment of release. Sack Number Two went flying off at a tangent. Up, up, up—and then a loud reverberating KER-WHANG.

In the silence that followed he could hear the thump of his heart.

"Good God awmighty!" Murphy bawled. "You missed!"

Jay-jay stared. He'd thrown hard enough, but not high enough. There it hung, his sack, Murphy's sack, the Marines' sack, dangling from the topmost strand of the barbwire vee like a lumpy over-inflated punching bag, far above his reach.

At that instant a shrill whistle from the direction of his truck split the night.

And then he heard a new sound that set all his juices churning, the unmistakable throb of a helicopter.

# TWO

"IT's THEM!" somebody said. "MPs!"

From the south an airborne light, not far above treetop level, surged steadily closer as it grew in brilliance. Frozen in his tracks, Jay-jay stared as though hypnotized.

"Jump, kid!" Murphy hissed. "Jump!"

Jay-jay shook off his paralysis and stammered, "I—I'll try." Positioning himself under the sack, he flexed his knees, sucked in a deep breath, and sprang. His hands clawed at empty air and he fell back to the ground with a jar that rattled his teeth.

Murphy cursed, a blasphemy new to Jay-jay's ears. "Run!" he roared.

Backing off once more, Jay-jay measured the height and hurtled forward. Momentum and sheer desperation added spring to his leap. One hand caught a grip on the chain link. His free hand reached out, groped, and made contact. With both hands he grabbed the sack and swung free of the fence. Fibers ripped and tore and gave way under his weight. With bone-shaking impact he fell on his back, stunned and bruised, the trophy clutched firmly to his chest.

"Come on, Murph!" a voice called. "Those chop jocks'll blow us down."

"Wait!" Jay-jay panted, as visons of dollar bills whisking away like autumn leaves flashed through his brain. "Wait!"

Staggering to his feet, he gathered himself for a supreme effort and heaved again. The sack arched up and over, spilling oranges and onions in its flight, and landed beyond the fence in the arms of Murphy.

Amazed at this double feat—both his own and Murphy's on the receiving end, a play action pass worthy of the Los Angeles Rams—Jay-jay could only stand agape. Murphy raised a fist, pumped it twice, turned, and hurried after his retreating comrades. Within seconds the Physical Fitness Field Exercise trainees had melted into the night like a gang of burglars with their loot.

Loot? Jay-jay suddenly realized he hadn't collected a dime. Not one red cent.

Still in a state of semishock, he peered back at the toyon clump a hundred impossible yards uphill across open ground, then at the oncoming helicopter. Its searchlight, a baleful yellow eye, probed the earth and fence below its belly in a relentless sweeping pattern. He felt as naked as a streaker on a beach, exposed and helpless. Every revolution of the whirling blade seemed to bring disaster one heartbeat nearer.

Glancing about wildly, he eyed the uninviting inky tangle of Las Pulgas Creek. Nettles and thorns? Poison oak? Creepy crawlies? Rattlers? Without further reflection he raced to the bank, plunged down over crumbling clay, and wormed into dense brush. Face down, holding his breath, he lay motionless.

The beam swept over him. Engine racket thundered in his ears. Prop wash fanned his hair. For one horrendous second he feared the bird was swinging back to make a second pass. Maybe the MPs had spotted a loose orange where none should be. Maybe they would land in the clearing to investigate, or radio for help. But no, they continued on course, sound and light gradually diminishing.

In the sweet soothing after-silence Jay-jay mopped the sweat off his face, longing for a gallon of ice-cold anything to sluice down his throat. Never had he valued peace and quiet more. Murphy and the MPs back to back had almost done him in. Presently he rolled over and sat up. Some hustler you are, he told himself. From now on stick to gardening.

He twitched at the sound of a soft low whistle from above, then a voice whispered, "Is that you, Jay-jay?"

Carla was peering down at him from the bank. "In the flesh," he said. "Thanks for the warning."

"My pleasure," she said. "Are you okay?"

"Swell. Fine and also dandy."

"What are you doing down there?" Her voice held a note of concern.

"That's what I keep wondering," Jay-jay said. "Ready to go home now?"

"Any time. Did you get your money?"

He shook his head. "Things happened too fast. I even forgot to ask."

"It serves you right. But I'm sorry, anyway." Carla leaned forward and pointed. "What's that?"

"What's what?"

"Behind you, that shiny thing."

Jay-jay turned, hauled out his flashlight, and directed

the beam at a section of tubular corrugated steel piping about two feet in diameter. Almost concealed by brush, it lay on the creek bed and led, tunnel-like into the earth underneath the fence. He crawled to the mouth, which was covered by a security grating. When he poked it with a finger the rusty, corroded mesh gave way like a rotten window screen.

Gingerly Jay-jay poked his head into the opening. At the far end, some thirty feet beyond, he made out a small circular patch that had to be the exit. Powdery gray silt coated the bottom. "Culvert," he said. "I never noticed it before."

Carla skidded down the bank and knelt beside him. "A culvert?" she said. "For this dinky dry little creek?"

"Wait until next rainy season. Some years, it's a gusher."

"But where does it go?"

"Where all creeks go. To the ocean. Right spang across Camp Hobart T. Pennington."

"Oh." Carla pinched her lower lip and gave him a long appraising look. "Jay-jay, are you thinking what I think you're thinking?"

"Why not?" Emboldened by this discovery, he felt a renewed sense of purpose. What am I? he asked himself. A jellyfish? I have my rights same as anybody else.

"That's crazy," Carla said.

"Look," he told her, "those guys can't be very far yet. They're holed up over there real close. Wolfing my food. For free."

"Suppose you find them and they won't pay off? Suppose you get clobbered. Suppose—"

"You're a ray of sunshine, you are," Jay-jay said.

"Think of it as a challenge, Carla. A business risk. If I'm not back in thirty minutes—"

"No way! You're not leaving me behind again."

"Who's going to watch the truck?"

"Truck, cluck," she said. "You'll need a witness. If you go, I go."

"Over my dead body."

"Try and stop me!"

She snatched the flashlight from his hand, pushed him aside, and squirmed into the culvert. "Quit that," he said and grabbed for her ankle, but she jerked free and crawled beyond his reach, humping along like a hyperactive glow worm. With a sigh of resignation he ducked his head and crawled after her.

Carla was waiting at the other end, just inside the fence, crouched on the creek bottom. She snapped off the light and handed it back. Jay-jay straightened, beat the dust out of his jeans, peered over the bank, and listened intently. He had expected, or half-hoped, to hear sounds of merriment, an orgy of finger licking, lip smacking, jaw crunching, and loud belching. Murphy and his crew would not be dainty diners. But there was only the hoot of an owl.

"Where are they?" Carla whispered.

"Dunno." A short distance downstream the clearing ended in a tangle of trees and brush that appeared big enough to hide a regiment. This hadn't been such a peachy keen idea, Jay-jay now realized. Marines were masters of camouflage and concealment; they made their living at it. But having come this far he was not about to turn tail and slink away without a token gesture. Not under the cool sardonic eyes of Carla Zink. "We'll take one quick gander, then call it a night."

Climbing from the bottom and stepping softly, he led the way. Behind him Carla moved as stealthily as a TV Indian in warpaint. They stopped, went on, and stopped again at the edge of the woods. He heard the rustle of a breeze among the leaves but nothing else. This close up the massed growth looked impenetrable, almost menacing. His nose caught an aroma of skunk, blended with the smell of eucalyptus and decaying vegetation. The place had an air of desolation, as though no one had invaded its privacy for years.

"Not even Marines could eat that much food so fast," Carla said.

"They probably took off in another direction," Jay-jay said. "We lost 'em. You've had your scenic tour. Let's go back."

"Aren't you curious?"

"Curious? About what?"

"This—" Carla swept a hand toward the trees. "It has such spooky vibes! Can't you feel them?"

"I feel some vibes about that MP chopper. Come on."

As though on cue the slap-slap-slap of a blade swelled across the night. He saw the onrushing light, seized Carla by the hand, and pulled her into the thicket. They floundered ahead a few yards and hit the dirt. After what seemed an interminable wait the helicopter passed overhead and flew on.

His heart still pounding, Jay-jay stood up slowly and blinked to get his bearings. Beside him Carla uttered a cry. "Look! I see something."

"Where?"

Without answering she pushed deeper into the jungle. Jay-jay drew a breath and followed. There was no path. They had to grope their way, dodging branches and low boughs, detouring around cactus and snarls of head-high chaparral. Carla glided through it all, confident and unscratched, while he bumbled and stumbled and tripped over roots. And then she halted so abruptly that he bumped against her.

"Jay-jay, a house!"

He stared, made out a solid shape in the blackness ahead, and played his light on it. Carla's "house" was an abandoned roofless hut partly overgrown by creeper, with a single empty eye of a window and a yawning doorway. The brown adobe bricks flecked with straw, melted by time and the elements, looked as ancient as the Pyramids of Montezuma. Rusty cans and cigarette butts—those artifacts of modern man—were conspicuous by their absence.

"Nobody's been here for ages," Carla said.

Jay-jay stepped closer and peered inside. One small square room. Bare earthen floor. No remains of human habitation. In one corner a pack rat's nest of twigs. Dust and cobwebs and overall a faint indescribable odor that Jay-jay associated with caves.

"I'll bet the Marine Corps doesn't know this place exists," Carla said.

"Could be." Camp P, he knew, went back some forty years, to World War II. Before that it had been a vast cattle ranch, dating much further back to the days of land grants. Before the Civil War. Before the Gold Rush. Before the gringos came. "Likely some Mexican cowboy lived here," Jay-jay said. "Water from the creek. Beef on the hoof. Grew a few beans and greens. He had it made."

"What do you suppose happened to him?"

Jay-jay smiled at her. Clearly Carla had a story teller's imagination, inherited from Daddy. "Nothing romantic. He lost his land. Those slick Yankee lawyers grabbed it for taxes."

"How do you know so much?"

"Grandpa Gribben's grandpa owned a hunk of it once," he said. "Aunt Hattie has the last five acres."

A section of the hut's rear wall, that side nearest Las Pulgas Creek, had collapsed, spilling a huge mound of disintegrated 'dobe onto the floor. Maybe undermined by floodwaters long ago, Jay-jay guessed. Noticing a pale object protruding from the pile, he crossed the room and knelt. Carla dropped to her knees beside him. "Jay-jay, wait," she said. "Are you superstitious?"

"Black cats and gypsy curses?"

"No. What I mean is—psychic. I have the weirdest sensation."

"Me too," he said. "I'm hungry. I'm thirsty. I'm bushed. What sensation?"

"You'd just laugh and make a dumb remark."

He gave the object a gentle tug, pulled it free, and suddenly his scalp tingled as if plugged into an electric circuit. The thing was dead white, bone white. It *was* a bone. Slender, almost weightless, somewhat enlarged at both ends. A shin bone. "Ulp!" he said.

"I told you so!" Carla clapped her hands together. "I knew it."

Jay-jay stared at the bone, then at Carla's rapt face, and licked his lips. "It's human. I think."

/ 23

"Naturally," she said. "I'll help you dig."

Together they scooped away loose dirt and more bones tumbled out. Some he could identify: a thigh, an arm, ribs and toes and finger bones. And, finally, a skull. The jaw structure and teeth were intact but the top (cranium?) was pitted with holes and cracks. The cavernous eye sockets stared at him accusingly.

Jay-jay tapped the flashlight, whose batteries seemed to have developed tired blood. A dead man, he thought. Or dead woman. But how did he (she) get here? When? Why? And, especially, what? What am I going to do about it?

"It's a skeleton," Carla announced.

"Yeah, I noticed," he said. "Part of one anyhow."

"Your Mexican cowboy must have died and his friends buried him here."

"*My* cowboy? How do you bury anybody in a 'dobe wall?"

"Maybe his body lay here undiscovered and the wall caved in and covered it," Carla said. "Either way, it's sad."

Jay-jay gave the light another shake. The bulb was definitely dimmer. "Funny about that skull," he said. "It looks human but then it doesn't."

Carla brushed a fingertip over a bulge above the eye sockets. "Deformed, isn't it?"

"Sort of. And look at that jaw. He must've been a chinless wonder."

At that moment the flashlight gave up altogether, leaving them in darkness. Blackout. Jay-jay fiddled with the switch to no avail. With my kind of luck tonight, he thought, that figures.

"We can't leave him here like this," Carla said, unshaken.

"Why can't we?"

"Because it would be—unchristian," she declared. "Indecent. We'll bury him again."

"Dig a grave? What with, our fingernails?"

"Then we'll take him with us. Bury him at home."

Jay-jay groaned. All this and Carla too. So humor her, he told himself. Anything to crawl out of this snake pit. "Peace be with you," he said.

With her jacket and his they managed to bundle up all the bones in two packets and tied the sleeves. Not quite like Christmas wrapping but it would do. In silence, each bearing some mortal remains of Mr. or Ms. X, they filed out of the hut. Peering back, Jay-jay had an eerie sensation of his own: Sooner or later he'd be seeing this place again. Maybe in his dreams.

The return journey through the thickets, up the slope to the fence, and through the culvert was uneventful. No chopper. No MPs. No Marines, hostile or friendly. Only the black brooding night which seemed to muffle all sound. When they reached the truck Jay-jay dug an orange crate out of the back and dumped the bones into it.

Twenty minutes later he pulled up in front of Carla's house. The light was still on. To his immense relief he heard the machine gun rat-a-tat-tat of Daddy's typewriter. "Doesn't that man ever slow down?" he said.

"He's a demon at the keyboard," Carla said. "Thanks for everything, Jay-jay."

"You're welcome, I'm sure. About that ten bucks—"

"I'll mark it down in my little black memory book," she said.

"Don't forget your bones," he reminded her. "Not everybody has a cemetery in the backyard."

"You bury them. I don't have a shovel." With that parting message, Carla slipped out of the cab and wriggled her fingers at him. Running up the walk, she disappeared into the house.

Wearily Jay-jay drove back to the Flea Farm. He stowed the orange crate in the tool shed, climbed to his room, and flopped into bed, beset by physical and emotional exhaustion. Some night! he thought. You set out to earn a few dollars and wind up with a box of gen-u-wine Camp Pennington souvenirs. There ain't no justice nowhere.

# THREE

Jay-jay woke up about noon and had to struggle a moment to orient himself. His room. His hideaway. His retreat from a sometimes baffling world.

The tower, erected more than half a century earlier by Grandpa Gribben, no longer served its function of storing water from a well. Water to irrigate the farm now came through pipes from a river hundreds of miles away. But the great redwood tank, empty and unused these many years, still stood on the platform that formed the ceiling of Jay-jay's room.

Descending the ladder, he entered Aunt Hattie's house. Hattie, who regarded all motorized vehicles as contraptions of the devil, was out delivering fresh eggs on her bicycle cart. Jay-jay showered, dressed, prepared a large brunch, and mapped his strategy for the remainder of the day.

His immediate chores—feeding the chickens and mulching the flower bed—took some while. Next, he picked a crate of cucumbers and a lug of tomatoes on order from his best customer, a health food store in Hilldale. The gas gauge in the truck registered low but not critically so. Enough fuel left for one round trip.

At four-thirty that afternoon Jay-jay presented himself at the main entrance gate to Camp Pennington, sweaty palmed but determined, and inquired for Master Sergeant Moose Majeski. An MP in the control booth asked for some ID, made a series of phone calls, and at length issued him a visitor's pass. Jay-jay drove between rows of barracks and quonset huts and at last located the Senior Noncommissioned Officers' Club.

The sergeant was waiting at the door, a cigar clamped between his teeth. In his khaki uniform, chest ablaze with campaign bars, Moose looked even more formidable than Jay-jay remembered from their one previous encounter. On that occasion Moose, then in civvies, had stopped by the farm seeking a likely recruit for his game plan. "Hi ya, kid," he said breezily now and gave Jay-jay a cruncher of a handshake. "You got a problem?"

Jay-jay managed a watery smile. "Money."

"Join the crowd," Moose said. "In this outfit it's always thirteen days till payday."

"That's the trouble," Jay-jay said. "I wasn't. Paid, that is. Last night."

"That jarhead Murphy didn't pay off. Why not?"

Jay-jay explained why not.

When Jay-jay had finished describing his trauma of the helicopter Moose threw back his head and brayed with laughter. "No sweat," he said. "I'll collect from Murph when he comes draggin' in tomorrow. He owes me a bundle. Here." He produced a billfold, whisked out five twenties and tucked them deftly in Jay-jay's pocket.

Jay-jay colored and transferred them to his wallet.

"You figured maybe old Moose would welsh on the deal?" Moose gave him a conspirator's wink. "Well, my feelings don't bruise easy, kiddo. Not when we got our private gold mine in them thar hills."

"Gold mine?"

Moose stepped forward and opened the door to the club. "Look."

Jay-jay saw a huge room fitted out with tables, lounge chairs, and a bar. Tobacco smoke, beer fumes, the din of voices and loud laughter filled the air. The senior NCOs, sergeants all, from three stripers up to six, were at ease after a day on the rifle ranges and drill fields of Camp P.

Moose let the door swing shut and, with a pipe wrench grip on Jay-jay's arms guided him back to the truck. "Get the idea now?"

"No," Jay-jay admitted. "Sure a lot of sergeants though."

"Tip of the iceberg," Moose said. "Every lard butt on this base is tagged to run that survival course. You and me, we got us a steady supply of customers. Gilt-edge guaranteed."

"You want me to do it *again*?"

"Now listen good," said Moose, lowering his voice. "We got a new CO, commanding officer to you, a two-star general bucking for three. Hell on wheels for fitness. He fires a fresh batch through every week. That totals up to four hundred bucks a month for you, kid. And," he added virtuously, "a little extra take-home pay for me."

"But, Moose, you told me this was a one-shot job. To win a bet."

"Was. But now we have a brand new ball game. It's money in the bank."

"Well, uh, thanks. I'll think it over," Jay-jay said. *A two-star general? Hell on wheels?* Breathing fire and brimstone? Not for four *million* a month. Thanks, but no thanks. Take your marbles, chum, and get out of here. But one question he had to ask first. "Moose, do you know anything about an old adobe hut back in the brush? Near the creek?"

"Hut?" Moose frowned. "Never heard of one and I served two hitches on this cow pasture. What about it?"

"I found some odd-looking bones."

"Human bones? A skeleton? Inside the fence?"

"Outside." Jay-jay lied, for reasons obscure to him but which, at the moment, seemed prudent. Nor did he mention Carla Zink. "It was awful dark in there. But they could be."

"Bones, huh?" A change seemed to come over Moose. His eyes squinted. He took a long pull on his cigar and rubbed his chin. "Tell you what, Jay-jay. I'll ask around. Meantime, keep your lip buttoned. This is strictly between us. Right?"

"Right." Jay-jay slid behind the wheel and started the motor, eager now to escape. "Nice doing business with you, Sergeant."

"Likewise. But you ain't seen nothing yet." Moose gave him another wink. "So long, pardner."

Pardner? Jay-jay thought as he drove away. Moose and me? Never again. But those bones rang a bell with him. He acted funny. Funny peculiar. Did I open my big fat mouth once too often?

After the hurly-burly of Camp P the main street of Hilldale, self-proclaimed Avocado Capital of the World,

30 /

seemed almost deserted. Jay-jay filled his gas tank at a service station and then delivered his cucumbers and tomatoes to the store, an establishment called The Elemental Seed. The girl behind the counter informed him there was a message.

Jay-jay scowled at the note: "Dowser, call Huff Realty. Urgent."

"Urgent?" he said. "How long ago did this character call?"

"Early this morning," the girl told him. "How come he calls you here instead of home?"

"A long boring story," Jay-jay said. "And I'm stuck with it. But thanks for the word."

He returned to the pickup and drove across town, hoping the office would be closed and the parking lot empty. Maybe he could postpone this till another day. But a solitary car, a bronze Mercedes, occupied the head honcho slot, signaling the after-hours presence of P. Martin Huff. That's my man, Jay-jay thought. Persistent. P as in *pest*.

P. M. Huff, alone at his desk, looked up with a smile. "Sit down, sit down," he greeted Jay-jay. "You're a hard young fellow to contact. Always on the go."

"I'm sorry, Mr. Huff," Jay-jay said. "But the answer is still no."

"Well now, let's not be hasty," the realtor said. "High time we had a friendly chat."

"No use, Mr. Huff. My Aunt Hattie won't budge. She's a strong-minded woman."

A small, mod-dressed man, Huff had agate eyes and a drawstring mouth adorned by a mustache. According to gossip he was slicker with a dollar bill than Houdini.

"Whenever I phone," he said, "she hangs up on me. Returns my letters unopened. You know what happened last time I tried to reason with her."

Jay-jay repressed a grin. On that occasion, some days past, when Mr. P. M. Huff had come calling in person, checkbook in hand, Hattie had turned to the manure pile, which Jay-jay replenished weekly from the Hilldale Riding Stables, and pelted him with horse apples. His dignity wounded, Huff had retreated and kept his distance since.

"Look at it this way, Jay-jay," Huff said. "You and I, we represent our community. Want to see it prosper and grow. But your auntie, that misguided lady, is blocking progress."

"I don't follow you."

Huff rose from his chair and stepped to a land tract map on the wall. The tract, outlined in black grease pencil, was subdivided into a mosaic of squares, rectangles, triangles, and other varied shapes, studded with a rainbow of thumb tacks. A gap near the center, as yet unnumbered, looked familiar to Jay-jay.

"My firm," Huff said in his solemn organ tones, "owns all this property or has options to buy. Except one piece."

"The Flea Farm?"

"Precisely." The realtor handed him a pamphlet. "Here's our new brochure."

Jay-jay stared at an artist's visualization of what surely must be Heaven on Earth: an expanse of rolling green lawns, a lake, a golf course, stately palms. Beautiful young couples sailing boats, riding horseback, playing tennis. And, smack in the middle, a dazzling white building not much bigger than the Pentagon. A poor man's dream of Paradise.

"That's the clubhouse," Huff said.

"Clubhouse?"

"Right where your farm is now. A marvel of modern development. Read it."

Phrases swirled before Jay-jay's eyes: ". . . prestige country estates . . . overlooking the blue Pacific . . . gracious living . . . luxury ranchos . . . sun-kissed days and balmy nights . . ." Then he peered at Huff. "You're going to turn all those hills and brush into this?"

"A vision of tomorrow," Huff declared. "Azure Acres. Poetry in action."

"It doesn't overlook the blue Pacific," Jay-jay pointed out. "Even on a clear day."

The realtor shrugged. "The point is, Jay-jay, I've made your aunt a generous offer. She can't afford to turn me down."

"She already has."

"That's where you come in. You're a bright young man, her only kin. She'll listen to you. So, you persuade her to—"

"She won't sell that land to you, Mr. Huff, or to anybody. She's lived there all her life. Where would she go?"

"Move to town. Into one of those retirement homes. Miss Gribben's no spring chicken."

"Retire? Aunt Hattie?" Jay-jay shook his head. "Not a chance."

"You have to think of her welfare, your own future," Huff went on. "I like your style. We could work together. How'd you like to sell real estate?"

"I don't guess," Jay-jay said.

"With a new car the day you start. How does that grab you?"

"You're offering me a job and a new car," Jay-jay said, "if I talk Hattie into selling. That's it?"

The realtor clapped him on the shoulder. "In this cold world you have to look out for Number One."

"I can't do it, Mr. Huff." Jay-jay stood up. "Have to go now."

"Don't get on your high horse, sonny." Huff's smile clicked off like a master switch. "There might be a bonus in this for you."

"For some gracious living?"

"This town needs Azure Acres. It'll bring in big money, more jobs, a wider tax base. A lot of important people are backing it."

"They should've asked Aunt Hattie first. When the farm's for sale she'll call you."

Huff's face reddened. "Don't play cute with me, Dowser. No dotty old hag is going to foul up my subdivision."

Jay-jay dropped the brochure on the floor and walked out.

As he drove north from Hilldale through the winding valleys, past the lush hillside groves, Jay-jay wondered if he should have been more, uh, tactful. Huff was said to be a wheel in county politics, have some clout in high places. He might be able to stir up trouble. But that crumb! Jay-jay thought with renewed outrage. Trying to bulldoze Hattie off her land.

The weather had changed, he noted. Dark clouds were massing over the mountains and the evening air had a tingly electric feel, as though a rare summer storm were on the way. So let it pour. Sun-kissed Azure Acres could always use more rain.

Dust billowed behind when he swung off the pavement

onto the dirt road that led toward home. Bone dry, he thought. Which reminded him of Carla Zink and the ten dollars he'd promised her. As he slowed in front of the Zink place the unceasing beat of Daddy's typewriter drifted from an open window. The time seemed unripe. Jay-jay rattled on across Las Pulgas Creek and turned into the farm.

He stared at his surroundings, attempting to picture a palatial clubhouse. A golf course. Artificial lake. And all those bright beautiful prestigious people. *Poetry in action.* Where did Aunt Hattie fit in?

Jay-jay found her by the fertilizer tank, mounted on an overturned tub stirring the contents with an old canoe paddle. He pecked her on the cheek, said, "Hey, good lookin', what's cookin'?"

"Don't you jolly me, Jay-jay Dowser," she said crisply. "Where've you been all afternoon?"

"Chasing the almighty dollar." He decided not to burden her with the latest details of Huff's subdivision. Aggravation enough for one day. The tank contained a thick, brown evil-looking liquid. He leaned close and pinched his nose. "Whew! Something new's been added."

"It's a special formula," Hattie told him. "Super Fortified Vitamin Vigor, I call it."

"Super Vigor?" Jay-jay said. "That stuff should grow hair on a pool ball."

"Bosh." Hattie laid aside her paddle and gazed at the heavens. "Leo is in ascendancy. The stars never lie."

The eastern sky had turned plum purple, trailing a curtain of rain over the high peaks like the fringe of a giant shawl. A breath of cool moist air brushed Jay-jay's cheeks. "You, the stars, and the Weather Bureau," he said.

Hattie sniffed. "Those dodos and their gadgets. Jay-jay, go fetch the rods."

He walked into the tool shed and gathered an armload of ten-foot steel construction rods, the kind used for reinforcing concrete. Hattie was into something she called "electro-culture," a process he did not pretend to understand. The theory, she'd explained, was to apply atmospheric electricity to stimulate plant growth and crop yield. To Jay-jay it smacked of sorcery.

By the time he returned, Hattie was on her knees in her plot, transplanting what appeared to be tangles of roots from a flat into the earth. With her trowel she scooped out a hole, popped in the roots, patted back some dirt, and heaped the remainder into a mound. Her hands moved swiftly, deftly, nonstop, as if she were playing some delicate musical instrument.

Jay-jay watched in admiration. "What are those? Turnips?"

"Creets," said Hattie.

Aunt Hattie aspired to follow in the path of her idol, Luther Burbank, the plant wizard, who had given the world such wonders as the spineless cactus and seedless prune. For the past few months she had been attempting to cross a carrot with a beet to produce a hybrid "creet." Jay-jay, who hated beets and was not that ape for carrots, lacked her enthusiasm but loyally supported her efforts. "What color do you suppose they'll turn out?" he said.

"No matter," she said. "They'll be nutritious. And delicious."

He cocked his weather eye. The storm front was closing in rapidly, blotting out the skyline. Lightning flickered, followed by a distant rumble of thunder. A raindrop splatted on his chin. "Looks like a lulu," he said. "Where do I stick these?"

"Here." She pointed with her trowel. "And there. And there."

It took Jay-jay only a minute or so to place the bars upright in the soft dirt about six feet apart, forming a circle of mini–lightning rods. Then he stepped to the tank and slopped several buckets of Super Fortified Vitamin Vigor over the fresh mounds of creet plantings.

"That's enough," Hattie said. "We mustn't overdose the little darlings."

"They'll sure get baptized tonight," he said and turned up his collar as the rain began in earnest. "Let's go before we're soaked."

Another bolt of lightning streaked across the sky as they hurried to the house and more thunder crashed, this time much closer. Jay-jay washed up at the sink and was toweling off when Hattie thrust a book at him. "If you're still a doubting Thomas," she said, "read this. Page 72."

It was the *Organic Gardener's Almanac.* Jay-jay skimmed over the passage she had underlined. ". . . gardeners frequently make use of metal posts to take advantage of the local magnetic fields . . . relationship between plants and electrostatic energy . . . electro-stimulation . . . root energizer . . ."

"Far out," he said. "It's scientific, not black magic."

"The planets," Hattie said loftily, "affect all life on earth, including plants."

Jay-jay crossed to the front window and peered out into the gray dripping dusk. "By the way," he said, "what happened to that crate of bones in the tool shed?"

"That was very thoughtful, Jay-jay," she said. "Sometimes you do remember."

"Remember what?"

"How much I needed them. The price of bone meal what it is nowadays. Scandalous."

"But I didn't bring those bones for you. They belong to Carla Zink."

"That little snippet down the road?" Hattie harrumphed. "She couldn't grow dandelions."

"Carla may not be the Green Thumb Wiz," Jay-jay said, "but—" and then he had a delayed reaction. Bone meal! "Aunt Hattie, you didn't—"

"Yes I did," she said. "Ground them up in the pulverizer. Just what the doctor ordered."

"You—you—" Jay-jay gulped for breath. "You mashed them? The skull? Those leg bones, finger bones? A human skeleton?"

"Bones are bones," Hattie said. "All that lovely calcium and phosphate. Ashes to ashes, dust to dust, earth to earth, that's what the Good Book says."

Jay-jay struggled to regroup. "You crunched 'em up? you dumped that guck in the fertilizer tank, into your Super Vigor, and now—"

His voice broke off as another peal of thunder rattled the windowpane.

"Don't you fret. Your Aunt Hattie wasn't born yesterday." She gave his ear an affectionate tweak. "Good night, dear. I have to go work on tomorrow's horoscope."

# FOUR

JAY-JAY BREWED A pot of tea and whipped up an omelet for his supper, all the while weighing what he would say to Carla if she asked about the missing bones. Not if, he amended, when. Carla was that kind of girl. Furthermore, he suspected that she would be shocked and angry if he told her the truth. She'd entrusted the bones to him.

When the rain let up he ran across the yard and climbed to his room under the water tank. Even on the wettest wildest night he felt snug here. Secure. Peeling off his clothes, he flopped into bed, undisturbed by the storm outside. The patter of raindrops on his rooftop reservoir lulled him to sleep.

Some while later he jerked awake and sat up abruptly when another bolt of lightning struck. It threw his room into lurid relief and lit the sky with a blue-white glare. He could smell ozone, almost taste electricity in the super-charged air. Close, too close for comfort! he thought and waited out the rolling, booming thunderclap.

His eardrums ringing, Jay-jay padded to a window and peered into the night. His aunt's bedroom window remained dark. It was almost as if Hattie Gribben, after consulting the Zodiac, had ordered this storm per schedule and then slept through it. Maybe the Weather Bureau could take lessons from her.

Should I climb down there, he asked himself, and make sure she's okay, check the place out? Check it for what? Tramp around in the mud? She's all right, I'm all right, he thought. Go back to bed, Dowser. You're a growing boy and need your rest.

The rain had stopped. The only sound was a steady drip of water from the eaves. But he became aware of a smell that had replaced the ozone—the rich ripe smell of fertilizer, super strong now, almost sickening. Jay-jay burrowed under the blanket and closed his eyes once more. If nothing else, Aunt Hattie had stunk up Azure Acres to high heaven.

Jay-jay's alarm clock, the red rooster down by the chicken pen, woke him early. He rolled over to catch a few more winks but his conscience nagged him into action. Yawning and stretching, he peered out the doorway. Bright sun bathed the hills in golden light. No fog or smog, no scud of cloud, marred the clear blue sky. Liquid diamonds sparkled on the brush. Among the trees a mockingbird ran through its repertoire.

Nobody, but nobody, he vowed to himself, is going to slice this farm into a cruddy subdivision. Not if I can help it.

After breakfast he stepped out into the yard, testing for smell. The fertilizer stench had dissipated during the night, except for a trace that still lingered on the fresh cool air. At that moment Carla appeared. Dressed in halter and shorts today, she didn't seem as skinny as Jay-jay recalled.

With those long muscular legs she looked like a track star, say, a high hurdler.

"Morning," she said. "I was afraid you'd still be in bed."

"Not us tillers of the soil," he said. "Up with the dawn." From his wallet he pulled out a ten-dollar bill. "I meant to stop by yesterday but your father was busy."

"I didn't come for the money," Carla said, "but thanks. Can I borrow a few eggs? I ran out."

"All you want. Fresh from the factory."

"And a little coffee?"

"Coffee's one of Hattie's no-no's," he said. "Tea we got."

"I'll settle for that. And can you spare a loaf of bread?" She turned her head, crinkled her nose. "What's the funny smell?"

"Barnyard special," Jay-jay said. "Let's go see."

Carla followed him across the garden along a path between rows of vegetables and fallow plots, dodging puddles of rainwater left by the storm. As they neared the fertilizer tank Jay-jay stopped abruptly. Stared in disbelief. Of the steel rods he had planted the evening before, encircling Hattie's creets, not one was standing. They lay scattered about like so much scrap iron.

What had been a tank was now a shambles of kindling—junk. The stout oak staves, split and splintered and charred. The hoops a twisted molten mass. The spigot a fused shapeless hunk of metal. Umpteen gallons of fertilizer blown sky-high. As if some nut, some fanatic with a grudge, had set off a bomb.

"What happened?" Carla asked.

Jay-jay stared at the mounds of newly planted roots,

which appeared mucky but undamaged. It wasn't raining rain last night, he thought. Or daffodils. It was raining Super Duper Vigor, Hattie's latest brew. Had her experiment worked? It must have worked! Right on target. There was no other explanation. Only she hadn't figured on such a powerful blast. He burst into laughter.

"What's so hilarious?" Carla demanded.

"We got zapped," he said. "A hundred thousand volts. Give or take a few."

"That's good?"

"It's called electro-culture. But Hattie underestimated Old Lady Nature." Briefly Jay-jay explained the principle.

"Lightning kills people, you know," Carla said. "Suppose you'd been here when it hit."

"Maybe I'd be turned into a pumpkin," he said. "Or a creet."

She laughed. "Which reminds me, where did you bury those bones?"

"I didn't."

"Why not?"

Jay-jay sighed. This gal had a one-track mind, bones on the brain. He could probably trust her with a secret but Hattie came first. If word spread around the countryside that Aunt Hattie, widely regarded as a weirdo, was grinding up bones, maybe human bones—no, he couldn't tell Carla.

"Maybe," she said, "we should set up some kind of marker."

"A tombstone? Carla, you—" His train of thought derailed. "Hey!" he exclaimed. "Over there!"

"Dowser, you're stalling."

"No, I'm not. Look." He pointed to a set of bare human footprints which, in his preoccupation, he had failed to notice earlier. They led across an empty field into the brush. "We had a visitor last night."

"Maybe one of your hungry Marine buddies crawled under the fence," Carla said.

The prints, deep and evenly spaced in the moist black loam, were smallish to medium, about a size 6, Jay-jay estimated. Fresh, recent, very recent, made within the past few hours, most likely by some kid. "Must be that Torrance brat," he said. "Lives up the road. I caught him twice last spring ripping off our oranges. Thought I'd scared him away for good."

"The one called 'Tuffy'?" Carla's brow creased. "A ten-year-old child, wandering around alone at night, in a thunder storm? With no shoes?"

"To know him is to loathe him. Spoiled rotten. That's our Tuffy." And then Jay-jay had an inspiration, a providential, ready-made explanation. A little white fib. "Sure, he has to be the one. Tuffy snitched those bones. Out of the tool shed where I left 'em."

"Stole them? Why would he do that?"

"Who knows what goes on in his itty-bitty brain."

"He must be some kind of ghoul," Carla said.

Jay-jay gave an elaborate shrug. "Well, no big loss. But I better make sure he didn't swipe the family jewels."

He followed the footprints to the edge of the field, lost them among the rocks and dripping brush, then backtracked to the citrus and 'cado grove. He made a hasty inventory of the shed, searched the truck, and circled the house. Nothing. No missing tools, no apparent damage or vandalism. So why had Tuffy been prowling around? If, in fact, it had been Tuffy. But now, Jay-jay was trapped in his own spider web of invention.

When he returned to the tank he found Carla poking among the debris. "I've been thinking," she said. "If lightning helps plants to grow, why wouldn't it help animals? Or people?"

"People *are* animals," he said. "And it fries 'em to a crisp. You just reminded me."

"You needn't be so grisly," she said. "But it does make me wonder. I'll ask Daddy—"

Anxious to divert her from the missing bones, Jay-jay said quickly, "Better not keep him waiting for his breakfast. I'll go round up some eggs and stuff."

"Jay-jay." Carla lifted her dark, long-lashed gaze. "I don't usually go around borrowing groceries."

"What are neighbors for?" he said, "You did me a favor the other night."

"That was different. I'd pay you now but, the truth is, I—we—Daddy needs that ten dollars. We're kind of short till he finishes his book. A lot of back bills and—"

"Pay me? Carla, forget it."

"But you've been honest with me. You see, Daddy—" She hesitated, seemingly about to explain further, but some restraint held her back. Embarrassment? Jay-jay wondered. Pride? Then she gave him an enigmatic smile and said, "Never mind. Some things bug me, that's all."

Minutes later, watching her stride down the road with a sackful of fixings, he speculated, and not for the first time, about Walter Zink. Everybody—well, nearly everybody—had money shorts and unpaid bills now and then. That might explain the rundown Zink house and yard,

Carla's concern for a buck. Beyond that, though, there was something strange about Daddy. Definitely. What really bugged Carla?

As Carla crossed the bridge a car drove past her from the other direction, toward the Flea Farm. A light-colored sedan, Jay-jay noted absently. And then he observed its blue dome. The law. And for no specific reason he felt a tremor of apprehension.

The driver pulled to a halt across from the mailbox, nodded, and called, "Would you be Dowser? Julian Jerome Dowser?"

Jay-jay crossed to the cruiser. "Jay-jay for short," he said. "Something wrong, officer?"

The officer stepped down, a compact man in a wrinkled uniform with a gun belt buckled around his waist and a clipboard in one hand. "Hoyle, deputy sheriff," he said.

Jay-jay bobbed his head. His voice seemed stuck in his windpipe.

Deputy Hoyle, regarding him at length in silence, finally said, "You mind telling me where you were last night, Jay-jay?"

"Last night? Asleep. In bed."

"What time did you get up?" the deputy asked. "Roughly."

Jay-jay swallowed. No questions about the night *before* last night. "The usual time," he said. "Around six-thirty."

"Jay-jay, you happen to own a wig?"

"A WHAT?"

"Wig. W-i-g. You know, a hairpiece." Hoyle tapped his head.

"No, sir!"

The deputy sighed. "We got a screwy complaint," he

said. "Screwy but serious. There's this nurse who works the graveyard shift. She's driving home four o'clock this morning when she jumps some creep in the middle of the road. Front of your place."

"What kind of a creep?"

Hoyle referred to a sheet on the clipboard. "I give it to you in her words. Quote: 'I was driving slow because the road was slippery. Then I saw this—this creature standing there, peering into my headlights. He wasn't very tall, with long stringy hair, stooped shoulders. Not one stitch on. When I jammed on my brakes he leaped into the brush and disappeared.' "

"Not . . . one . . . stitch—" Jay-jay repeated the words as their significance sank in. "Naked?"

Hoyle nodded soberly. "Naked. That's what the lady says. Jaybird naked."

"It sure wasn't me!"

"I'm not accusing anybody," Hoyle said. "Just making inquiries. Got any ideas?"

"Maybe he belongs to a nudist colony," Jay-jay offered.

"Not in this county," Hoyle said. "We closed 'em all down."

Jay-jay considered the nurse's description: not very tall, long stringy hair, stooped shoulders. Fit that together with the footprints in the garden and you got—what? "I'm not accusing anybody either," he said. "But you might check out a kid named Torrance."

"Why?"

"Just a notion. He's the neighborhood pain."

Deputy Hoyle jotted a note on his clipboard, asked a

few more questions, said thanks, then climbed back into his cruiser, and drove away.

Farther along the still muddy road Jay-jay located a set of tire skid marks, and beyond them a row of footprints leading into the chaparral. It was clear that Tuffy or someone else had stopped and then jumped for safety, probably scared out of his skull. After a few minutes Jay-jay abandoned his search for further clues and returned to the farm. *Screwy but serious*, Hoyle had said. A creep. That's his problem, Jay-jay thought; not mine. I got enough already.

He found Hattie, bright-eyed and pert, serenely contemplating the results of her electro-culture experiment. "Jay-jay," she said, "we need a new fertilizer vat."

"They don't make them like that any more," he said. "A new one would cost a mint, Aunt Hattie."

"How true." Hattie's gaze traveled over the farm and came to rest on Jay-jay's quarters in the water tower. "But we might move that old tank down here and use *it*."

He paled. "The water tank? It's forty times as big. Holds four thousand gallons!"

"Yes, dear." She gave him a dreamy smile. "Just think how much fertilizer we can mix up then."

Next day Jay-jay put in one of his longer stints at physical labor. He weeded the vegetable garden from end to end. He cleaned the chicken pen and pruned the lemon trees. By six that evening he was tired, but pleasantly so, glowing with a sense of virtue. Nothing like some sweat and honest toil, he told himself, to take your mind off all the hassles.

Then he heard the hum of an approaching motor. A military jeep swooped into the farm and skidded to a halt. Sergeant Moose Majeski stuck his head out, peered back at the road, then said, "Kid, any place I can park this heap outta sight?"

Mystified, feeling fresh prickles of alarm, Jay-jay said, "Over in the grove."

Moose drove on and disappeared. Out on the road a large dark sedan slowed almost to a stop at the turnoff, then accelerated and took off again. Only then did Moose reappear on foot from the avocado trees. Resplendent in purple slacks and a yellow tank top with *Semper Fi* lettered across the chest, he looked bigger than Shamu the whale. "You get a look at those guys following me?" he asked.

"No," Jay-jay said. He couldn't imagine anyone foolhardy enough to follow—much less catch up with—Sergeant Majeski, in broad daylight or the darkest night. "You trying to hide from somebody?"

"Brother, you don't know the half of it." Moose rubbed his enormous hands together until the knuckles cracked. "Looks like we could have us a real bonanza."

"Uh, Moose, look—" Jay-jay moistened his lips. "About that Operation Survival, I don't think—"

"Forget that. Chicken feed. Kiddo, if we play this one smart we'll be up to our crotch in clover."

"Crotch?" Jay-jay blinked. "Clover?"

"Lemme see those bones," said Moose.

"What bones?"

"The ones you told me about. You found by the creek that night."

"Oh, *those* bones." Jay-jay sniffed the air. The fertilizer smell had gone entirely. He wished devoutly that he had left the bones in their rightful resting place, but it seemed rash to explain to the Moose just now. "Are—were they worth something? A bunch of old bones?"

Moose produced a horrible smug smile. "Let's check 'em out first."

Jay-jay drew a long breath. "As a matter of fact—"

"Come on, come on, we gotta move fast before word gets around."

"What happened was," Jay-jay began, "night before last—"

Moose's smile froze in place. "Something happened to our bones?"

*Our* bones? Jay-jay thought; but how come I get all the headaches? "We had a prowler," he said, wondering if a fib came easier the second time around. "Some kid. He swiped them."

"Some kid, huh? And you know him, right? Don't just stand there, Dowser. Throw your tail in gear and we'll go grab 'em back."

"Too late," Jay-jay said. "The cops are onto him already. Since yesterday."

"Cops!" Moose covered his face with both hands. His shoulders sagged. For one dreadful moment Jay-jay was afraid the sergeant might burst into tears. "Those bones—" Moose seemed to have trouble breathing. "You got any idea how much I—we can sell 'em for?"

"Not now you can't," Jay-jay said. "So don't tell me."

"Fifty big ones, kid. Fifty gees. Right down the drain."

"Fifty thousand dollars?"

Moose nodded.

Jay-jay looked over toward the no longer existent fertilizer tank and felt like crying himself.

# FIVE

At that moment Aunt Hattie took charge. Emerging from the house, she rang a hand bell and called with her customary vigor, "Jay-jay, supper's ready. Invite your friend. Wash up first."

Startled, Moose said, "Who's that?"

"My aunt," Jay-jay told him. "Better do like she says."

"I don't want supper!" Moose protested.

Like a stern country schoolma'am who would brook no disobedience, Hattie rang her bell again. "Come along, boys. Don't let the food get cold."

Muttering to himself, Moose trailed along to the house, where Jay-jay mumbled introductions. The sergeant towered like a giant sequoia over Aunt Hattie, which abashed her not one bit. She led him to the table and ladled out a generous portion of the evening meal, a broccoli casserole. There was a platter of radishes and sliced cucumbers, oven-fresh bread, a pitcher of iced tea, and, for dessert, cookies.

Moose ate with relish, although in uneasy silence, now and then darting glances at Jay-jay.

All the while Hattie kept up a cheery monologue on topics dear to her heart, such as weather, crop rotation, and non-toxic insect sprays. But presently, as a gracious hostess, she turned attention to her guest. "Mr. Majeski," she said, "that's a pretty shirt you're wearing."

Moose—to Jay-jay's amazement—blushed. "Thank you, ma'am," he said.

"When I was a schoolgirl," she went on, "I studied Latin. *Semper Fidelis*, if I translate correctly, means 'Always Faithful.' You must be a member of the Marine Corps."

Moose admitted that he was.

"When were you born, Mr. Majeski?"

"Beg pardon, ma'am?"

"The month, day, and year of your birth, please. And the approximate hour, if possible."

Moose supplied what statistics he could, adding that he'd never been told the precise hour of his arrival in this world.

"Which makes you a Leo," Hattie said. "Leo the lion. Strong and courageous, but sometimes crafty and devious. That's your nature, Mr. Majeski."

Moose, suddenly converted into a lion, sat nonplussed.

Hattie rose from the table, crossed to her desk, consulted a wall calendar, then returned with a small red book. She ran her finger down a column of figures and jotted several notations on a pad. "Interesting," she said. "In your near future the signs indicate a large sum of money. Very large. Are you expecting an inheritance?"

Moose opened his mouth but no sound issued.

"But," she continued, "I see forces gathering to stop

you. Powerful and dangerous forces. Your strength will not prevail. You must use your cunning."

"Uh—ma'am—Miss Gribben—"

Aunt Hattie bestowed her most tender smile upon him. "Come again soon, Mr. Majeski. Good night, boys. Have to do my homework. Don't stay out too late, Jay-jay dear."

The bedroom door closed behind her.

Moose scowled at Jay-jay darkly. "How did she know about the money? I'm asking you, Dowser."

"She didn't," Jay-jay said. "She doesn't. She reads the stars."

"Stars! I don't buy that shinola. You told her."

"Told her what?" Jay-jay said. "I don't know from nothing. You're holding out on me, Moose."

Once again the sergeant's expression underwent a chameleon change, from suspicion to a toothy grin. "That's right, kid. I am. For your protection. Believe me. Now, are there any more bones where you found the first batch?"

"Could be," Jay-jay said. "I didn't have that much time to look."

"Let's me and and you go look again. Now. Before dark."

"After dark. Too risky in daylight."

"But you said—"

"I lied a little." It was Jay-jay's turn to grin. Tit for tat, even Steven, sauce for the goose, and all that jazz. "For your protection. Believe me."

Moose stared at him for another long moment. "If that's how you want it. But, kiddo, you better be pretty-please-with-sugar-on for this one. We're talking about real money."

Two hours later, with dusk deepening into night, Jay-jay and Moose climbed aboard the truck. Briefed on the mission ahead and Carla's role in the previous one, Moose had changed from his gaudy threads into a more practical set of USMC fatigues, which he kept stashed in his jeep. He looked as out of place on the farm, Jay-jay thought, as a rogue elephant in a pet shop.

Moose had scouted the road for several hundred yards in either direction to make sure no would-be "followers" lay in wait, and he insisted now that Jay-jay drive without lights. To Jay-jay these precautions seemed excessive but he went along with them. Crossing the bridge, he coasted to a halt in front of the Zink house. Light glowed behind the curtained windows and Daddy's typewriter kept up its endless tattoo.

Jay-jay reached for the horn, reconsidered, then stepped down. "Won't be a minute," he told Moose.

"I don't see why we need a dame," Moose complained. "The more people in on this—"

"She goes," Jay-jay said, "or I don't."

He tapped lightly and, after a pause, knocked. The door opened on its chain and Carla looked out. "Hi," he said. "How'd you like to make another recon? Same price, in advance."

Carla peered beyond him at the darkened truck. "No," she said.

Jay-jay fished a bill from his wallet and held it to the light. "Twenty," he said. "Tonight you'll just watch. I have company."

"Who?"

"You'll like him a lot," Jay-jay assured her.

"I bet." Carla eyed the twenty, studied Jay-jay's face. "You really need me, don't you?"

"Absolutely. I'm counting on you, Carla."

"Well, just once more. This is positively the last time." She took the bill and returned a minute later with her jacket and a bandanna tied over her hair. "Good night, Daddy," she called and shut the door.

"How's he doing?" Jay-jay asked.

"Terrific. He's into Chapter thirteen."

At the truck Jay-jay performed more introductions, to which Carla responded with a frigid nod. Moose grunted a monosyllable.

Once on the rough narrow track that twisted alongside Las Pulgas Creek, Jay-jay switched on his headlights and crawled ahead cautiously. No vehicle had come this way since the rain, which had laid the dust and heightened the pungent scent of sage. The brush on either side seemed to have grown closer overnight. In total silence they rode to the edge of the clearing.

Why am I doing this? Jay-jay asked himself. To help Aunt Hattie raise money for her taxes? To pay the bills? To fight off P. Martin Huff and his subdivision? Yes and yes and yes. But mainly, Jay-jay admitted, because I can't resist the lure of fifty thousand dollars. Do I believe Moose and his nutty talk? No. But nobody believed Christopher Columbus either.

Here we go for broke.

He rubbed his sweaty palms on his jeans and said, "You ready, Moose?"

"What're we waitin' for?"

"The next chopper," Jay-jay said. "Carla, keep a sharp lookout. If anything goes wrong, take off."

"Something's wrong already," Carla said. "But I'm a sucker for a sob story."

Jay-jay inserted fresh batteries in his flashlight, handed a second light to Moose, then dug out two shovels and a pair of gunny sacks from the gear in the back of the pickup. Creeping out of the toyon clump, he and Moose entered the clearing in bright moonlight. No overcast tonight. No security blanket of fog and smog. Only the crystal heavens overhead. Perfect for stargazing astrologers, maybe, but not for two guys sneaking into no-man's-land.

For all his size Moose moved with the agility of a big cat, gliding from one bit of cover to the next. He's a master at this, Jay-jay thought, a pro who knows his job. But somehow I have to match him at his own game, on his own turf.

As they neared the fence Moose said, "Is this where you unloaded the chow?"

"Right over there," Jay-jay said and then stiffened as Carla's whistle pierced the night.

"What the—" Moose growled. Jay-jay grabbed him by the sleeve, spun him toward the creek and gave a yank. Together they tumbled down the bank. Within seconds he heard the racing slap-slap-slap of a helicopter and, seconds after that, the searchlight swept past, a blinding dazzle that surely must reveal them to the MPs above. Only when the racket had dwindled and the light faded did Jay-jay release his breath.

"A squeaker," he said. "I told you we'd need Carla."

Moose raised his face from the dirt. "For a dame she sure can whistle Dixie," he conceded.

"How much time do we have till the next flyby?" Jay-jay asked.

"Maybe an hour." Moose said. "But they don't run on schedule like a bus."

On his belly Jay-jay wriggled down into the creek bed and snapped on his light. Just ahead, two minute buttons caught the beam and reflected it back. He grinned as a bullfrog let out a chuggerrum and leaped from sight. Too bad for those hungry Marines, he thought. Frog legs, a gourmet goodie.

Through the ruin of the grating Jay-jay peered into the culvert with dismay. Its roomy circumference had been reduced by at least a third. The storm and sudden runoff had deposited about a foot of silt on the bottom of the tube. His tunnel, his one access route into Camp P, had shrunk alarmingly.

"Not so good, Moose," he said. "Tight squeeze. Unless we dig some."

"Frig that," Moose said. "Move out, kid. You wouldn't believe the stinkin' hellholes I bellied through in 'Nam."

With his flash in one hand, shovel in the other, Jay-jay wormed forward. Two nights ago he'd had room to spare, plenty of space in which to maneuver. A piece of cake. Then. But now, tonight, he felt trapped, entombed, like one of those spelunkers—cave explorers—crawling into the bowels of the earth. The mud seemed to have hardened, compacted into 'dobe brick, as though determined to block his passage. The deeper he penetrated, the narrower the culvert appeared and the slower his progress.

What's that fancy word? he wondered. *Claustrophobe?*

A guy who goes bananas when shut in a small dark place. Like a disease. I hope I don't catch it.

"How much farther?" Moose panted, close behind him.

"Halfway," Jay-jay said, his voice echoing eerily. "You okay?"

"So far. We have to come back the same way?"

"Yup. Unless you brought some clippers to cut the fence."

The sergeant cursed.

Jay-jay paused to rest and wipe the sweat out of his eyes. The air was hot and humid and smelled faintly of garbage. Several feet ahead he made out some debris washed down by the creek: rusty cans, a tennis shoe, a half-eaten watermelon rind. Then he heard a squeak. Rat, he thought. That's all we need. Rats. Rats and another rainstorm, a flash flood boiling through here like the LA Aqueduct. A dandy place to drown.

Inching ahead again, Jay-jay spied a pale ellipse that marked the culvert's other end, his escape hatch. Then he became aware of Moose's labored breathing, no longer at his heels but farther back. Over his shoulder he called, "Come on, we've got it made."

"Can't." Moose swore. "I'm stuck."

"Stuck?" Jay-jay said. "How?"

"I'm wedged in like a cork!"

"Wiggle free."

"Wiggle? You loony kid, I'm froze solid!"

"Moose, you gotta try harder! Suck in your gut."

Moose's reply would have blistered paint.

Jay-jay shut his eyes. Think your way through this one,

Dowser, before that whirlybird zooms back. The MPs can't see underground but they may come equipped with sensors that detect body heat. *My* body. "Hang loose," he called. "I'll have you out in no time."

Jay-jay slithered out of the culvert onto forbidden soil, stood erect, and sucked in several quick deep breaths. Peering about in the moonlight for inspiration, he saw nothing to give him aid or comfort. Nothing but the wrong side of a ten-foot fence. Safety lay only a few steps away, beyond the wire, but it was now as unreachable as Jupiter.

Resolutely Jay-jay willed himself to crawl back into the pipe and squirmed forward until he came head to head, face to face with an apoplectic Moose Majeski. The sergeant's predicament, he saw at first glance, was critical. Mass versus friction, no doubt. Moose had plugged up the culvert, sealed it tight, with his own two-hundred-fifty-plus pounds.

"Shine that light outta my eyes!" Moose snapped.

Hastily Jay-jay obliged. "Why don't you crawl back backwards," he suggested. "You know, roll your butt, dig in your toes—"

"Arrgh!"

"Let's try this." Jay-jay put a hand on each of Moose's shoulders, braced himself, and pushed with all his strength. And pushed. And pushed. And gave up in exhaustion. So welcome to Camp Pennington, he thought despairingly. Moose can't get in. I can't get out. Checkmate. "I'll think of something," he said.

"Sure you will," Moose said. "You and your crappy ideas."

Crawling in reverse, Jay-jay worked his way to the outside world once more. More than half an hour had elapsed since the last chopper pass. When was the next one due? Stepping to the fence, he whistled twice, the emergency signal he'd agreed on with Carla.

Presently she came slipping across the clearing. "Trouble," she whispered. "I knew it. Where's your fat pal?"

Jay-jay gestured with his thumb. "Down there. Stuck."

"No strain," Carla said heartlessly. "Let him starve a week or so. That should do the trick."

"What about me? Do I starve too?"

"I'll smuggle you a bag of munchies every night," she said. "What's your favorite brand?"

"Ha-ha and ho-ho." Jay-jay peered at her through the wire, feeling like the Prisoner of Devil's Island. Just how far *could* he trust this gal. "Can you tie any knots?" he asked.

"Dowser, I grew up on Mission Bay. On a boat. I can tie knots you never heard of."

"Swell. There's a rope in the back of the truck. A hundred feet. Now here's what you do—"

She listened, nibbling on her lower lip, until he finished explaining his plan, then shook her head. "That's above and beyond the call of duty. Besides, it won't work."

"Why won't it?"

"Because I'd be too scared."

"Would the sweet smell of money stiffen your backbone?"

"It might," she said. "You must be made of the stuff."

"I'm not," Jay-jay said. "But I could be. How's about another fifty bucks, Carla, on the cuff? You willing to gamble?"

"That's a lot to ask."

"That's a lot of bread."

"Fifty?" Carla cocked her head to one side, a bird debating whether to peck or not to peck. "For that kind of money I could learn to love you, Jay-jay. But if I weren't so broke—"

"Exactly my sentiments," he said. This was going to be as tricky as a triple reverse, real dipsy doodle. But for the moment, by a fluke of circumstance, he had Moose at his mercy. In a bind. Over a barrel. Helpless. It gave Jay-jay a reckless, heady sense of power. He stuck two fingers through the fence and said, "Shake."

Carla closed her fingers over his and returned the pressure. "Shake," she said. "Do those chopper cops use live ammunition?"

"God willing," he said, "we'll never find out. Sit tight till I give the signal."

"Cheers," Carla said and melted into the night.

Staring at the foothills and the high black mountains beyond, Jay-jay waited anxiously until she disappeared. Not a light gleamed up among the steep rugged slopes. Empty country, lonely country, he knew, an island of wilderness surrounded by suburbia. Over the years more than one plane had crashed in the coastal range without a trace.

He thought of that now as a Navy jet screamed north at better than Mach I and five thousand feet, off the base at Miramar. Suddenly his pulse jumped. From the opposite direction came the MP chopper again, clattering along like a freight train at fifty feet.

Flopping into the creek bottom once more, Jay-jay pressed flat. Had Carla made it back to cover and the truck? Would she be spotted in the open? This time she hadn't whistled. He closed his eyes against the light and breathed a little prayer. If Carla got caught because of him— Any instant he expected to hear—dreaded—a yell, a bellow on a bullhorn, even a burst of gunfire.

If we squeeze out of this, he promised himself, NEVER AGAIN! Cross my heart and hope to die.

# SIX

THE CHOPPER SAILED on without pause, traveled off to the south along the fence. Silence closed in, a lovely absence of all sound. Jay-jay lay limp a few moments longer, rallying his forces, then switched on his light and crawled back into the culvert to confront Moose once more.

Time had not improved the sergeant's appearance or his smell. Sweat runneled down his cheeks and dirt caked his face. "Took you long enough," he growled. "Where you been?"

"Thinking," Jay-jay said. "About those bones."

"Screw the bones," Moose said. "Get me outta here."

"Sure thing," Jay-jay said. "Soon as you level with me."

"Level?" Moose's voice took on an injured note. "After all I done for you—"

"Oh, I'm grateful," Jay-jay said. "But it's getting late. Carla has to be home by twelve o'clock."

"What's she got to do with anything?"

"She pulls you out or nobody does, that's what. You want to spend the night here? Let the MPs nab you tomorrow?"

"That scrawny babe is gonna pull me out *how?*"

"She's strong for her size," Jay-jay said. "Start talking, Moose. The bones."

"You two smartie pants wouldn't try to hornswoggle old Moose?"

"You said it. I didn't. Time's a'wasting."

Moose swiped a hand over his eyes and gave a grunt of resignation. "Okay, okay. You know what the Peking Man is?"

"Peking, that's in China," Jay-jay said. "The capital."

"Yeah. Well, the way I heard it, an American scientist, a long time back, fifty years or so ago, dug up some skeletons in a cave outside the city."

"Who'd you hear this from, Moose?"

"Different people. After you mentioned finding bones I asked around camp. Old-timers, civilians, here an' there. Anyway, I got the dope. Those bones are half a million years old."

"Half a *million!*"

"Close enough," Moose said. "The Chinese put 'em in a museum. Big deal. But during the war, around Pearl Habor time, somebody stole 'em. Been missing ever since. The government—that's the Commies now—offered a reward to get 'em back."

Jay-jay studied Moose's hooded eyes for some clue to his emotion. Guile? Deception? Could Moose Majeski invent a yarn like this on the spur of the moment? Not likely. Ancient bones. A long-ago war. A museum in forbidden mysterious Peking. An unknown thief. Reward. The combination boggled Jay-jay's mind.

Here I am, he thought, down this rat hole, listening to an Oriental fairy tale, and believing it! Almost.

"You satisfied now?" Moose said peevishly. "Go crank up that chick and let's blow outta here."

"You left out one detail," Jay-jay said. "Peking's seven thousand miles from Pennington. What's the connection?"

"That's all I know, kiddo. God's truth."

"Good night, Moose," Jay-jay said and started to back away. "See you in the brig sometime."

"Wait!" Moose clutched at his retreating arm and missed. "You wouldn't leave me behind, not your pard."

"Wouldn't I?"

Imprisoned in his metal cocoon, Moose pondered. "Awright, here's the scuttlebutt: A gunnery sergeant named Brown was stationed at the U.S. Legation in Peking. Marine Color Guard. 1941. Japanese Army invading north China. Big bustup."

"Sounds confusing," Jay-jay said.

"War ain't a picnic," Moose said. "Orders came down from the top. The Marines pulled out, guarding two footlockers full of Peking Man. They got cut off, never made it."

"Were they killed?"

"Naw, taken prisoner, the whole detail. But this Brown, he got the smarts, figured those bones might be solid gold, and stashed the lockers somewhere. A very cagey operator."

"A friend of yours, by any chance?" Jay-jay asked.

"Never laid eyes on him. He's long dead now."

"Then how do you know it's true?"

"Who's telling this story?" Moose demanded. "Anyhow, years later, after the war, he went back to China, dug up his loot, and smuggled it out to the States."

"And how," Jay-jay said, "did it turn up on Las Pulgas Creek?"

"Brown pulled his last hitch here on Pennington," Moose said. "Kind of a nut, they tell me, after prison camp and all. A loner. He didn't dare cash in his bones by then. He hid them again. Only way it figures."

Vas you dere, Charlie? Jay-jay wanted to ask. Now who's got the smarts? How could anyone learn the truth at this late date? And yet—and yet—the bones had been real. Somebody's bones, before Aunt Hattie ground them into meal. There just *might* be more buried in that old hut down the creek. "Who else knows about this?" he said.

"Nobody," Moose declared.

"You thought somebody followed you tonight. Why?"

"Because maybe some sharpie put two and two together and played a hunch. But nobody knows *where*. Just you and me."

"Let's hope," Jay-jay said.

He backed off again, out into the night, and scanned the southern sky for a helicopter. Perhaps forty minutes had passed since the last flight, which left a margin of safety. But how much? Moving to the fence, he flicked his flash on and off three times.

Over behind the toyons the pickup wheezed and coughed and finally caught. In the stillness it sounded louder than a cement mixer. Driving dark, Carla jockeyed the truck across the clearing down to the fence, then backed it to the creek bank, guided by Jay-jay's hand signals. Not bad, he allowed, for a girl who'd grown up on a boat. Not bad at all.

She hopped out with the coil of rope and whispered, "Is Fatso ready?"

"Ready as he ever will be," Jay-jay said. "Heave ho."

"He may lose some skin," Carla said.

"He can spare it. Go easy on the clutch."

Carla tied one end of the rope to the rear axle and disappeared over the bank. Jay-jay heard her crawling through the brush into the culvert. Then silence. He waited, watching the sky and mentally chewing his fingernails. Two minutes. Three. Four. What was going on down there? Was the rope long enough?

At last Carla returned. She dusted off her hands, gave the rope a vicious tug, and said, "It barely reached. He's got ankles like a rhinoceros."

"But a heart of gold," Jay-jay said. "Bombs away."

Carla climbed into the cab, revved the engine, and shifted into low. Through the fence Jay-jay looked on anxiously. The Ford found traction in the soft earth and inched ahead, pulling the rope taut. Then the rear wheels spun. The engine stalled. Fumes of gasoline and scorched rubber filled the air.

Round One to Moose Majeski.

Jay-jay megaphoned his hands. "Carla," he called, "next time pop it. Hit the pedal hard."

"Don't blame me if Lard Belly breaks your rope," she said and started the motor once more.

Gears clashed. The truck leaped forward several yards and stopped. Brush crackled in the creek bottom and the rope went slack. A large disheveled figure crawled over the bank on all fours. With a moan Moose hobbled to his feet and sagged against the fence. In the moonlight he looked a ghastly shade of green. "That dolly!" he gasped. "That little witch, she liked to peel my hide off!"

"You can thank her later," Jay-jay said. "Jump in the truck—"

They both turned and looked up as the all too familiar slap-slap-slap cut across the night. Carla, still behind the wheel, gave a whistle. The chopper's spotlight seemed to race toward them like a winged locomotive.

Jay-jay groaned. Oh no! he thought. Not so soon, not again! Give us thirty seconds more. Pulllease! "Carla!" he yelled.

Carla needed no prompting. She gunned the motor. With a roar the truck shot up the rise, wheels churning and tailgate banging. The rope, one hundred feet of stout manila, still bound securely around Moose Majeski's ankles, did not break. Nor did the knot jerk loose. Carla had tied it well.

Moose's legs flew out from under him. On his back, feet first, he went bouncing across the clearing like a dummy in an old-time Western movie, the bad guy dragged by a runaway horse. His voice, if any, could not be heard above the engine noise. Within seconds he and the truck vanished under the nearest stand of oak trees, leaving an empty stage.

Having witnessed this performance with gleeful wonder, Jay-jay dived into the creek again, the third time in as many hours.

It was almost midnight when Jay-jay walked Carla to her front door, said a brief good night, and saw her safely in the house. Then he returned to the truck and drove a battered unhappy Moose back to the farm. "We'd better swab some disinfectant on those cuts," he said.

"What I need," Moose grumbled, "is a quart of whiskey. But I don't guess—"

"Sorry," Jay-jay said. "You can sleep here tonight. I'll get some blankets."

"Sleep here? Me?" Moose looked at him in disbelief. "Dowser, did anybody ever tell you that you're a jinx? You and that girl, you're a double whammy."

"It wasn't all my fault, Moose."

"Maybe not. But there's got to be an easier way to make a buck." Unexpectedly Moose grinned. "No hard feelings."

Jay-jay shook hands. "If I find any more bones I'll phone you."

"You do that," Moose said, "and we'll both die rich." He limped over to the jeep, squeezed his bulk into the seat, and poked out his head. "Tell your Aunt Hattie she was right."

"Right about what?"

"That us Leos got a lot to learn. See ya, kid." With a blast of exhaust Moose barreled off.

Jay-jay eased into the darkened house, reinforced himself with milk and cookies, then wearily climbed to his room. It had, he noticed, a musty smell, as though it needed airing, which puzzled him because he left both windows open all summer for cross-ventilation. Maybe Hattie had been up here and spilled something. But what? And why? Hattie rarely came to the tower for any reason.

His brain spinning with fatigue, he collapsed into bed. Questions, questions. But no answers. Moose wasn't the only one with a lot to learn. As for Peking Man—in the quiet seclusion of his room Jay-jay's doubts returned. I just don't believe it, he told himself. 'Tain't possibly so.

Much later he was wakened from deep sleep by a noise. Raising his head from the pillow, he listened. What had he heard? A thump? A squeak? In his befuddled state he couldn't identify the sound or its source. He waited a minute and sank back. Maybe a skunk nosing around the compost pit. Or a stray cat on the prowl.

Then he heard it again, a muffled furtive noise from nearby, down in the garden. Wide awake now, Jay-jay threw back his covers and stepped to the doorway. For some while he peered into the night, studying shadows in the moonlight. Nothing moved. There was no further sound. It was that dead hour before dawn when all creation seemed wrapped in cotton.

Finally he gave up and padded back to bed. Imagination, he guessed. Or nerves. Probably he'd be hearing helicopters in his dreams for weeks.

Next morning he slept late, so late that Aunt Hattie joshed him mildly when he appeared in the kitchen for breakfast. "Early to bed, early to rise," she said. "Me oh my, the way you gallivant around at all hours."

Jay-jay laughed. "No way to get wealthy and wise, that's for sure. Did you hear me drive in last night?"

"Slept like a log," she declared.

"I don't suppose you heard any other noise later," he said. "Around four?"

"Such as?"

"I'm trying to place it. I was so punchy—" Jay-jay reconsidered the problem as he spooned down his cereal. Footsteps he ruled out. A cry, a voice? Something to do with the mouth? He took another swallow of granola and then he had it. "Like an animal eating," he said. "Gnawing food. Bite, crunch, chaw, like so." Jay-jay demonstrated. "Maybe bones."

"Bones!" Hattie, busy arranging roses from the flower garden, set down her vase. "If some varmint's been raiding my hen house—"

"Big Red would've sounded off," Jay-jay said. "But we'd better go look."

They hurried out together and found the chicken pen intact. Also the melon patch. Likewise the tomatoes. But the carrot plot—the carrots that Hattie used for her creet experiments—had been decimated. Something had pulled up the better part of two rows, bitten or torn off and discarded the feathery tops. A few pulpy stubs lay scattered about.

"Heavens to Barbie!" Hattie exclaimed. "What kind of critter eats like that?"

"A gopher maybe," Jay-jay said. "Or a raccoon." The something, whatever it was, apparently had devoured the carrots on the spot and spat out the less tasty parts. Munch, crunch, chomp. As ravenous as a Marine.

"More like a hog," Hattie said. "Must have gobbled twenty pounds."

Jay-jay hunted about for paw or footprints in the dirt but saw none. Two days of August sun had baked out all surface moisture. He picked up a stub and examined it. Then came enlightenment. "No hog ate these," he said. "I should've guessed."

Hattie stared at the teethmarks. "I do believe you're right, Jay-jay. They're human. But who in tarnation—"

"I've had it with that Torrance kid!" Jay-jay said. "Twice this week he's been mooching around."

"That little boy up the hill? But surely his parents can afford to feed the child."

"They oughta keep him chained up nights." Jay-jay strode across the yard and jumped into the truck.

A mile up the road he stopped at the Torrance mailbox. Beyond the fence a half-acre of manicured lawn stretched to a sprawling modern house. Whatever the Torrance tribe might lack, it wasn't coins. As Jay-jay marched up the flagstone walk a puzzler occurred to him. Why would a rich kid like Tuffy go for carrots? Probably the little monster lived on burgers and pop. But carrots, twenty pounds of carrots? Unless he had some rabbit blood.

A tiny warning gong pinged in Jay-jay's head just as he pushed the buzzer. A buxom woman in white opened the door. "Mrs. Torrance?" he asked.

"I'm the housekeeper," she said. "Mrs. Torrance isn't here."

"Is Mr. Torrance at home?"

"Mr. Torrance is gone too," the housekeeper said.

"How about Tuf—" Jay-jay recalled Tuffy's right handle, "Howard? He around?"

"The whole family," she said with a touch of impatience, "is away. On vacation. Hawaii. They left last month."

Jay-jay made one more feeble stab. "But Tuffy, he must be here."

"You're mistaken," the housekeeper said and shut the door.

Dazedly Jay-jay returned to the pickup. In the hot midmorning sun he felt a shiver ripple between his shoulder blades. Where are you, Tuffy, when I need you? In far-off Hawaii, the lady said. Left a month ago. So who *did* eat those carrots? Who *did* slink around the Flea Farm naked and leave his tracks? Some sickie with a warped sense of humor?

Jay-jay debated whether to call Deputy Sheriff Hoyle. And report what? *Yes sir, Officer, the nudist struck again. Left his teethmarks this time. No sir, Officer, I don't have any more bright suggestions. I goofed on Tuffy Torrance. Sorry about that.*

Somehow, Jay-jay told himself, I don't think that deputy has any sense of humor, warped or straight. So, when in doubt, stop, look, and listen. Use that sieve you call your brain. There has to be an answer, and you're the genius who has to find it. Fast.

# SEVEN

WHEN JAY-JAY RETURNED to the farm two cars were parked beside the house. One he recognized. The other, a coupe with an official-looking decal on the door panel, he did not. His mood switched from anxiety to slow-burning anger.

P. Martin Huff, the realtor, attired in a safari suit and lizard skin boots, stepped from his bronze Mercedes. "Morning, Jay-jay," he said. "How goes the produce business?"

"So-so," Jay-jay said. "What are you doing here?"

"I rang the bell," Huff said, "but nobody answered, so I took the liberty of waiting. No objections, I hope."

Aunt Hattie, Jay-jay knew, was out on her delivery rounds. Probably Huff knew that too and had timed his visit accordingly. "Mr. Huff," he said, "like I told you before, you're wasting your time. Why don't you leave us alone?"

The smile of P. Martin Huff did not waver. "Let's overlook our little talk the other evening. Bygones are bygones. Frankly, Jay-jay, I'm here on an errand of friendship. Mercy mission."

You and who else? Jay-jay thought. He stared at a man, presumably the owner of the coupe, who at that moment crawled around the corner of the house on his hands and knees. The stranger whipped out a notebook and scribbled with his pen. "Who's your friend?" Jay-jay asked.

"Not a friend," Huff said. "An appraiser from the county tax assessor's office."

"So be my guest," Jay-jay said. "But who invited him?"

The realtor shrugged. "It's a matter of public record. Everybody pays taxes. But some people fall behind. Your aunt, I'm sorry to say, is one. In arrears. Maybe you didn't know that."

As bookkeeper for the concern of Gribben & Dowser, Jay-jay knew it all too well. Taxes. He and Hattie struggled to keep up, but each year the gap seemed to widen. Taxes on the farm went nowhere but up in a never-ending spiral. Two hundred dollars more last year. Five hundred this year. A battle you couldn't win for losing. "What's your angle?" he asked Huff.

The appraiser got to his feet and walked over to the water tower. He pounded on the shingled siding with his fist and made another entry in his notebook.

"My angle," Huff said, "is to help you folks."

"How?"

"Let's see." Huff consulted a slip of paper. "To date Miss Hattie is delinquent to the tune of eight-hundred-fifty-six dollars. Plus penalties and interest. Call it a round nine hundred."

Jay-jay felt his stomach shrivel. Nine hundred! Out loud it sounded positively evil. So what did you expect,

Dowser? he asked himself. Don't play ostrich. You shut your eyes and hoped the bogeyman would go away. Or that Santa Claus would drop down the chimney with a sockful of cash in the nick of time. Like an overstuffed old Saint Nick named Moose Majeski.

"And," Huff went on smoothly, "there's next year's tax to think about."

Jay-jay began to see light. "What I think," he said, "is that you brought this monkey out here to boost our taxes again."

"Why would I do that?" Huff said with an air of hurt innocence.

The appraiser finished his inspection, pocketed his notebook, and walked back to his car. "Any old time, Mr. Huff," he said. "Always glad to do you a favor." With a nod to Jay-jay he climbed into the coupe and drove away.

Jay-jay shook his head at the perfidy of it all. At this game, he thought, I'm a babe in the woods, a lamb among the wolves. "Cute," he said. "Very cute. The old squeeze play."

Huff rolled off clichés like an assembly line. "You can't fight city hall," he said. "If you can't lick 'em, join 'em."

Over Huff's shoulder Jay-jay caught a sudden glimpse of Aunt Hattie furiously pedaling her bicycle cart along the road, heading this way, for home. On a collision course. She must have seen Huff's car go by, he guessed, and feared the worst.

"According to law," the realtor droned on, "the county steps in and seizes delinquent property like this farm, for instance, and auctions it to the highest bidder. You follow my drift?"

But Jay-jay was no longer listening. Fascinated, he watched Hattie's silent approach. She pedaled into the yard, dismounted beside the Mercedes, and placed a finger to her lips. Hitching up her coveralls, she advanced with a soft determined tread on the back of the unsuspecting P. Martin Huff. "Boo!" she cried.

Interrupted in midsentence, Huff jumped and twirled around abruptly. He gave her a silly grin and stammered, "Er—ah—Miss Gribben, you startled me."

"Must have a guilty conscience," she said. "Fleecing more widows and orphans, are you?"

"We've had our differences in the past," Huff said. "But forgive and forget, that's my policy."

Jay-jay smothered a snicker and said, "Mr. Huff is here on a mercy mission. He wants to pay our taxes."

"Pay our taxes?" Hattie simpered. "How generous."

Huff shot Jay-jay a confused glance and shifted uneasily. "That's not exactly what I had in mind," he said. "But now that you're here, Miss Gribben, let's get down to brass tacks."

"Tacks and taxes, by all means," Hattie said. "Thank the gentleman, Jay-jay. Mr.—uh, what's your name again?"

"Huff. P. Martin Huff. President of the Hilldale Development Corporation."

"Goodness gracious, that sounds important," Hattie said. "You must be a busy man."

"I am." The realtor brushed his fingertips over his mustache and plucked a folder from his jacket. "I also happen to be the proud creator of Azure Acres."

"It's poetry in action," Jay-jay volunteered.

Hattie studied the brochure and dissolved into a syrupy smile. "When's your birthday, Mr. Huff?"

Taken aback, the realtor said, "My birthday? February ninth. Why?"

"It's written in the constellations." Hattie gave a cackle of delight. "Aquarius. A water carrier."

"A what?"

"That's your heavenly sign. Water." She sketched a wavy motion in the air. "That's why you're so generous and creative. An Aquarius through and through. Dear Mr. Huff—" She backed away. "Excuse me for a jiffy."

Huff cleared his throat with a nervous hack. "Miss Gribben, I don't believe you understand—"

Jay-jay held his breath. In her pointed hat and floppy galoshes, Aunt Hattie at that moment resembled some mischievous sprite sprung to life from a chewing gum wrapper.

"But I do," she purred. "Quite." She reached down and lifted one end of the garden hose coiled beside her flower bed. A nozzle was attached. With her other hand she turned on the faucet.

A stream of water drilled Huff in the mustache.

For a second he stood rigid, a look of comic consternation on his face, as though he'd been splattered by a custard pie. Then he pawed at his eyes and bellowed, "Stop that!"

Hattie opened the faucet full bore and lowered her aim to Adam's apple level.

Waving his arms, crimson with rage and futility, Huff retreated, slowly at first, then he made a break and ran for his car. Implacable, Hattie pursued him, spraying water up and down his backside like a fireman hosing down a blaze. He leaped into the Mercedes and cranked up the window.

"Aquarius!" she shouted.

Huff shook his fist. "You crazy old bag!" he yelled through the glass. "You'll pay for this. Pay and pay and—" With water dribbling off his chin he gunned away.

Shaking with laughter, Jay-jay stepped to the faucet and turned it off. "He'll never trust you again, Aunt Hattie."

"The feeling," she said, "is mutual. Imagine that scoundrel! Trying to steal the farm right under my nose. He is, isn't he?"

"More or less," Jay-jay said. "But he'll be back. He never gives up."

"I'll be ready for him." Hattie tittered. "I can't abide a pipsqueak with a soggy mustache."

After supper that evening Jay-jay got a sledge hammer and a coil of copper wire from the tool shed. Collecting half a dozen poles Hattie used for bean trellises, he sawed them into three-foot lengths and drove them into the ground at five-yard intervals. On this row of stakes, which extended along one side of the vegetable garden, from carrot plot to cabbage patch, he strung a taut trip wire about shin high. To the wire he tied several cow bells, relics of an earlier time when Grandpa Gribben had raised beef cattle.

A do-it-yourself burglar alarm, almost invisible after dark.

The Creep. That was how Jay-jay had come to think of

their elusive prowler. And if Creep comes back tonight, or any night, he told himself, I'll be the first to know.

But who was Creep, now that Tuffy Torrance had been eliminated as a suspect? Some character hired by Huff to frighten Aunt Hattie off her land? One of those back-to-nature hippies camped out in the boonies? A Marine Corps deserter? Or what? Jay-jay gave up. He'd run out of possibilities.

For a while after slipping into bed he willed himself to stay awake, listening for the clank of cow bells, prepared to spring to action. But there was only deep night silence and waning moonlight outside his window. He drifted off.

*The cave lay open before him, a black tomb-like vault that reeked of antiquity. Dr. Julian Jerome Dowser, famous scientist, stepped forward, guided by the flickering torches of his coolies. He bent down and from the dust of ages picked up a gleaming ivory object and held it aloft. A skull. A human skull.*

*"Eureka!" he cried in his moment of triumph. "After years of searching I have discovered Peking Man."*

*His assistant, who looked like an Asiatic Moose Majeski, bowed low and said, "Master, for this great feat all China will honor you."*

*A sudden earth tremor shook the cave. Rocks crashed down from above. Dust billowed up from the floor. Dr. Dowser dropped the skull and fled.*

Jay-jay awoke from his dream in a sweat and peeled back his blanket. He seemed to be roasting and shivering at the same time. The dream had been so real! The smell. The skull. The falling rocks. Almost a nightmare.

And then he heard a sound. Not imaginary now, but

*really* real. The sound of a rock, or something, thudding softly against the side of the tower. Jay-jay waited, his teeth all but chattering, then it came again. KER-THUNK. A rock, thrown not in anger, not hard. But hard enough to waken anybody in the room. Anybody who didn't need a hearing aid, or maybe an Aunt Hattie.

After that, nothing. Only silence.

He eased first to one window and the other and then to the open doorway, careful not to silhouette himself, but saw no sign of Creep below. Creep might be a hairy slob who pranced around bare but so far he'd been too wily to trip the alarm, or too lucky. So go catch him, Dowser. Don't stand here sniffing the midnight air. You know every square foot of this farm. Creep doesn't.

Jay-jay slipped into his sneakers, grabbed a flashlight, and, still in pajamas, quickly descended the ladder. For several minutes he stood in the tower's shadow, hoping to detect any movement or the faintest noise, while his impatience mounted. Probably Creep had seen or heard him and was lying doggo. The problem was to flush Creep out.

Starting at the north end, Jay-jay began a systematic search. Behind the tower. The front and back of Hattie's house. The hedge alongside the road. All the obvious places he had checked the morning after the storm. But now there were no footprints, none that he could find. Which raised another question: If Creep came only at night, where did he hole up during the day? Did he have a car or get about on foot? And why, for cryin' out loud, did he pick on the Flea Farm? What was the big attraction?

At the tool shed Jay-jay got his first lead. The door, which he'd closed earlier after putting back the sledge, was ajar a slit. Yanking it open, Jay-jay drew a tremulous breath and switched on his flash. Nobody home. But some-body—Creep, who else?—had moved the wheelbarrow out of alignment several inches, as though perhaps frightened off when looking behind it. Looking for what?

A twig snapped among the avocado trees. Jay-jay swung his light around. A dark figure, partially caught in the beam, jumped from behind a trunk and disappeared deeper into the grove. With a surge of elation Jay-jay took off in pursuit. I've got you now, he thought; you raunchy little carrot thief.

But Creep vanished somewhere in the wilderness of brush and boulders that bordered Las Pulgas Creek. Jay-jay halted at the edge and peered across at the opposite bank, where the track wound west to Camp Pennington. Beyond it lay Walter Zink's property. Was Creep making for Carla's house?

Then Jay-jay heard a sound that set his heart racing—the slow exhalation of breath, somebody winded and fighting for air. To his right. Close by. He shone his flash on a tangle of vines that had grown over the lower limb of an oak. Still no sign of his quarry. But the leaves were trembling ever so slightly.

Jay-jay reached down, groped, and came up with a rock the size of a baseball. "You there, under the tree, come out!" he ordered. "Slow and easy."

No response.

He took a firm grip on his rock. "I'm counting to five. One!"

The vines parted. Breathing heavily, a short slim man in a black suit and white shirt and tie stepped forward. An Asian, he had close-cropped gray hair, wore thick horn-rimmed glasses, and was fastidiously dabbing at his forehead with a handkerchief. "Mr. Dowser, I presume," he said.

"Right." Jay-jay stared in confusion. The Creep? This cool cat, crew-cut, senior citizen all duded up in clothes? "Who are you?"

"Permit me." The stranger neatly folded the handkerchief into his breast pocket and slid a hand inside his coat.

"Hold it!" Jay-jay said. "No fancy moves."

"None, I assure you," the man said calmly and gave Jay-jay a rueful smile. "As I discovered this evening, I no longer have the agility or endurance of youth." He presented a business card.

Jay-jay read it at a glance:

DR. EUGENE CHEN, PHD, SCD
CULTURAL ATTACHÉ
UNITED NATIONS MISSION
THE PEOPLE'S REPUBLIC OF CHINA

"My permanent post," Dr. Chen went on, "is director of anthropological research at the University of Peking."

"The Peking Man?"

"Indeed. Possibly I am one of his descendants. Several thousand generations removed." Dr. Chen gave a dry little laugh. "Mr. Dowser, if you can put aside your suspicions momentarily, I suggest that we proceed to a more congenial location and, as two citizens of the world, discuss matters of common interest."

"Who sent you, Dr. Chen?"

"My government. On a most urgent mission."

"Can you prove that?"

"Give me five minutes of your time. If you are not

convinced, notify the authorities." Dr. Chen smiled again. "I believe a reward was mentioned."

"Fifty thousand," Jay-jay said.

"The correct figure, Mr. Dowser, is ten times that amount. Five hundred thousand. Half a million dollars."

Jay-jay gasped. Dr. Chen had to be loopy, of course. Or lying through his dentures. Could there be that much money anywhere?

"Surprised?" said Dr. Chen. "You must understand, we Chinese revere our ancestors. Those remains are part of our heritage, a national treasure beyond price. We shall go to any lengths to recover them. But come—"

Jay-jay hesitated. *Any lengths.* That sounded like a threat. But Chen himself seemed harmless, if not exactly a true-blue, Eagle Scout type. So bounce the ball in his court, Jay-jay thought, and see how he swings. "After you, Doctor."

Dr. Chen led the way down into the creek bed and up the other bank onto the side road. A large sedan without lights was parked under the oaks. A second Chinese, a hulking bear of a man, sat behind the wheel. "My chauffeur and bodyguard," Chen said. "If I had not returned shortly he would have come after me. So I am not entirely helpless."

"Now I catch," Jay-jay said. "You're the ones who followed Moose Majeski here the other night."

"Very astute, Mr. Dowser. But we lost him, as you know, near your farm. So I decided to pay a return visit—"

"You think I have your bones?"

Dr. Chen coughed delicately. "Do you?"

"No."

"Very well. But I do think you have some knowledge. You see, this past week my associates have been investigating certain rumors at Camp Pennington. It came to their attention that one Sergeant Majeski was doing the same. Consequently they kept him under observation. And he led me to you."

Jay-jay found himself straining to pick up the background night noises. The hoot of an owl. The rustle of wind in the trees. The whine of a mosquito. Shifting position, he glanced back across the creek. He could almost feel the physical presence of something or somebody over there, concealed in the chaparral. "Dr. Chen," he said, "are you keeping *me* under observation? Some whacko staked out watching the farm?"

"Certainly not. Why do you ask?"

"Just curious," Jay-jay said. "I'm a Sagittarius."

"Ah yes, the inquisitive mind," Chen said blandly. "To your credit. Unfortunately our sergeant friend has a loose tongue. Indiscreet. Therefore I prefer to negotiate with you directly. No third party."

"Doctor, I never even heard of Peking Man till yesterday."

"So much the better. Exactly what did Majeski tell you?"

"Most likely lies," Jay-jay said.

"No doubt." Chen allowed himself another small laugh. "Would you care to learn the truth? Considering the sum involved?"

"Yes, sir, I guess so."

Dr. Chen reached out an imperious arm. Through the car window the bodyguard handed him a brown envelope, which Chen in turn passed to Jay-jay. "Our latest report," he said. "I recommend that you read it and reflect, then contemplate."

"But, Dr. Chen—"

"In due course," Chen said, "I will reestablish contact with you."

Jay-jay clutched the envelope and swallowed the phlegm in his throat.

"Good night, Mr. Dowser." Dr. Chen settled himself in the back seat of his limousine in august splendor. "May all your dreams be pleasant."

"Same to you," Jay-jay said and watched the car glide away and its taillights dwindle. Pleasant dreams, you betcha, to all you lovely people out there in Slumberland. Sugar plums, Tooth Fairy, the Sand Man. And leave us not forget Peking Man. What did I do, he addressed some nameless but omniscient deity, to deserve this?

# EIGHT

JAY-JAY ROSE EARLY, reread Dr. Chen's report carefully in the light of day, and put it aside for further reflection. Food for thought, but his investigation of the rock thrower had first priority.

Dressing quickly, he climbed down to the yard. Last night the rocks, or whatever, had bounced off the west side of the tower. A quick search yielded three black stones beneath the window. The stones were walnut sized, round, and smooth. Water smooth. The nearest water ran, on occasion, in Las Pulgas Creek.

Thoughtfully he jiggled them up and down on his palm. Who had thrown them? Who and why? Certainly not Dr. Chen or his bodyguard. Which left one and only one candidate: Creep.

Because he had no better place to look, Jay-jay headed for the creek. Starting at the bridge, he dropped onto the bottom and followed its winding brushy course downstream. What not so long ago had been mud was now dry clay. In places where the storm runoff had formed pools the surface was caked and cracked. With a stick he poked into potholes and tangled mats of roots, working his way along the boulder-strewn bed.

And then, at the foot of a sheer bank in the shade of a sycamore, he came upon a patch of sand. Here some animal had dug a hole about two feet across and perhaps as deep. On the bottom water shimmered. Several inches, an aquifer of subterranean water that looked clear enough to drink. Beside the hole lay a mound of smooth black stones.

On his belly, he scooped up a handful of water and sampled it. Cold. Sweet. Better than the chemically treated stuff that flowed through pipes. An animal? Jay-jay stared at his reflection. Animals dug holes, sure. But animals didn't collect stones. Animals didn't *throw* stones.

So what did that make Creep? When he, Creep, wanted a drink why didn't he turn on a tap or faucet like anybody else? Figure that one out, Dowser, and win yourself a blue ribbon at the County Fair.

Hurrying back to his room, he opened Dr. Chen's report, ten mimeographed pages stamped SECRET, and read it once again. It differed from Moose Majeski's scuttlebutt in detail but not in essentials.

For openers, Peking Man was not a single individual. In 1926 anthropologists unearthed the skeletal remains of forty persons—men, women, and children—part of a tribe or family group that had lived and died in the same cave. *Sinanthropus pekinensis.* The tallest was five feet one inch.

So, Jay-jay reasoned, there could be a lot more bones to recover. Maybe thirty-nine more skeletons. But it was the final paragraph that riveted his attention.

"Summary: Based on exhaustive investigation it is our

belief that these sacred relics were not lost or destroyed and do in fact exist. Our agents have conducted a worldwide search and are presently concentrating on Camp Pennington with hope of early success. Recent intelligence indicates involvement of U.S. Marine Corps personnel, now presumably deceased."

That last bit had a jolly ring, Jay-jay thought; real gallows humor. *Presumably deceased.* And who's next in line? That hotshot produce peddler, that part-time snoop, J. J. Dowser, who can't seem to mind his own cotton-pickin' business?

"Jay-jay!" Aunt Hattie's hail roused him from his reverie. "Are you up there, boy?"

He stuffed Dr. Chen's report among the dirty clothes in his laundry bag and went down to the yard.

Hattie was on her knees inspecting his burglar alarm. "What's this contraption?" she asked.

"To catch the prowler," Jay-jay said. "Or scare him off next time he pussyfoots around."

"He came all right," Hattie said. "Last night. But your dingus didn't work."

"You're telling me," Jay-jay said.

She rose to her feet, crooked a finger, and led him down the path. "There." Hattie pointed to some recently disturbed dirt at one end of the cabbage patch. "I counted them yesterday," she said. "Today six are missing. Six heads of my best Chinese cabbage."

"Chinese?"

"Crisp but tender," Hattie said. "Very tasty in chop suey. I don't begrudge a cabbage here, a carrot there, but this rascal must have a tapeworm for a stomach."

Jay-jay picked up a pale green leaf and stared.

"At this rate he'll eat us out of house and home," Hattie declared. "Think of something, Jay-jay."

He could not imagine Dr. Eugene Chen, cultural attaché, munching raw cabbage, Chinese or otherwise, in the dark of night. So, Creep again. Creep the nature boy and carrot lover, who threw rocks and dug holes in the creek bed. "He's probably hiding out," Jay-jay said. "From the law."

"Seems harmless enough. A mite tetched in the head. Hungry. And," Hattie added with approval, "he's a vegetarian."

"So was Adolf Hitler," Jay-jay said.

"I'd love to read his horoscope," Hattie went on. "He's a Scorpio, I'm sure of it. Creature of the wild."

"I'll ask him," Jay-jay said, "first time we meet up. Meanwhile, better keep your door locked nights."

"Balderdash." She pursed her lips. "There's an old French proverb: To catch a fly use sugar instead of vinegar. I have a feeling that he needs some milk of human kindness."

"What kind of kindness?"

"I'll show you this evening. Run along now, dear."

Jay-jay walked over to the scene of Hattie's electro-culture experiment. None of her creets had poked a sprout up through the earth. Maybe they never would. But as he gazed at the jumble of lightning-blasted staves and hoops he had a strange sensation. "Vibes," Carla Zink would call it. That bunch of junk was trying to tell him something. But for the moment the message escaped him.

After breakfast Jay-jay backed out the truck and drove down the track by Las Pulgas Creek. Several hundred yards short of his destination he parked under a sycamore and proceeded on foot. Never again, he'd promised himself. Never, but never. But now the situation had changed. Correction: If you believed Dr. Chen, it had changed.

He had to risk a second look at that hut. So why not try by daylight? Maybe the MPs patrolled only at night. Comforted by this analysis, he walked on to the toyon clump and sat down, well concealed, to eyeball the terrain.

Minutes passed. Birds caroled. Bees droned back and forth. Sun beat down from the cloudless sky. Beyond the fence, over on Camp Hobart T. Pennington, only a hop, skip, and a jump away, lay his target, the dark and silent creekside jungle. No human sound disturbed the morning calm.

Jay-jay grew antsy with impatience. If he waited much longer he'd lose what nerve he had. Satisfied that the coast was clear, he rose to his feet, about to dash for the culvert. Then he heard the rumble of an engine and ducked again.

A jeep pulled into view on the far side—the Marine Corps side—of the clearing and stopped. The driver leaped out, raced around to the passenger door, opened it, and snapped to attention. The passenger, a tall leathery man in fatigues and paratrooper boots stepped down.

Only then did Jay-jay notice a bright red license plate mounted above the front bumper. Emblazoned on the plate were—not numbers or letters—but two gold stars. Translation: a major general. Heavy brass.

Jay-jay stared. Was this Majeski's new CO, Hell-on-Wheels himself, the fitness fanatic? If so, what was he doing here, a two-star general? Could he be looking for those bones too?

The general raised his left arm to eye level and studied his wrist watch. Jay-jay held his breath. A countdown? Countdown to what? Or maybe the general was just admiring his watch. But Jay-jay suspected that Marine generals, this one anyway, didn't tick like ordinary mortals.

Suddenly the general reached inside his jacket, pulled out a whistle, put it to his lips, and blew.

The undergrowth across the clearing erupted with Marines, Marines in helmets and field packs, rifles at the ready. They charged into the open at a run, appearing almost magically. Fifty, a hundred, too many to count, an invasion out of nowhere. Jay-jay shuddered to think the unthinkable: Suppose he'd been over there, caught in the thick of it.

Somebody bawled an order. The rampaging Marines flung themselves to the ground, unstrapped entrenching tools, and began to dig. The crackle of small arms and machine gun fire broke out. A low-flying plane roared over, dropping smoke bombs. Two tanks trundled out of the trees and wheeled into position, their cannon snouts trained menacingly in Jay-jay's direction.

Through it all the general stood beside his jeep, immobile as a statue, observing.

War games, Jay-jay thought. They look real, they sound real, except that nobody gets hurt. Nobody except me. I'm the loser in this war. No bones today. Maybe forever. If Two Stars and his gang blast that hut—

Frustrated and disconsolate, he returned to the truck and drove home.

Seated by the telephone, Jay-jay spent the better part of an hour tracking down Moose Majeski in the vast complex that was Camp Pennington. When the sergeant's voice came on, it sounded wary and guarded. "Sure I'm okay," he said. "What's up, kid?"

"Can you talk?" Jay-jay asked, mindful of Dr. Chen's "associates." "Or is somebody listening?"

"On this line you never know," Moose said. "Any news?"

"Yeah, all bad," Jay-jay said, and described the maneuvers in progress down the creek.

"They're only shootin' blanks," Moose said. "So what's your problem?"

"The problem is, I can't go—you know where—until they quit. Knock off for the day."

"Kiddo, them there are combat Marines. Training. They don't work an eight-to-four shift."

"They fight at night too?"

"All night, all day, you got it," Moose said. "May go on for weeks. That new general, he's a sweetheart. Operation Slasher, he calls it."

"Weeks, huh, night and day?" Jay-jay tried to organize his thoughts. First, Operation Survival, now this. There would be no more sorties onto Camp P while Operation Slasher lasted. "Moose," he said, "do you know a Chinese named Chen? A professor from Peking?"

"Chen?" Long pause. "Not offhand. Peking, you say?"

"Peking," Jay-jay repeated. "Did you serve in China during World War II?"

"Me?" The sergeant laughed. "I'm not that ancient, pal."

"Chen knows you, or claims he does. He came here last night, looking for guess what."

"Don't mess with him," Moose said. "He's a Communist. A Red. I've been fighting them for twenty-five years."

"Maybe it's time to call a truce," Jay-jay said. "Who cares about his politics?"

"You can't trust a Commie," Moose declared. "I got two hunks of shrapnel in my hip to prove it. Tell him to drop dead."

"But, Moose—"

"Gotta go now. Take care, kid." And Moose hung up.

Was he lying? Jay-jay wondered. Or plotting some tricky double-cross? Or was he too scared to talk? If Moose is scared, what am I?

Arriving at the Zink house minutes later, Jay-jay was greeted by the zing of Daddy's typewriter. A shame to interrupt the man, Jay-jay thought, but this was an emergency. He tapped on the door, waited a decent interval, then knocked hard. Inside, the typewriter chattered on. He pressed the button but heard no ring. Probably busted. The third time he hammered with his fist and called, "Mr. Zink, is Carla home?"

Rat-a-tat-tat—

"Mr. Zink, can you hear me?"

Rat-a-tat-tat—

The man must be deaf, Jay-jay thought, although Carla had never said so. Or maybe he wore ear plugs. Jay-jay reached for the knob and turned it slowly. The door opened a few inches and stopped, held by a security chain. He put his eye to the crack, said, "Sorry to bother you, Mr. Zi—"

Nobody there. Empty room.

Rat-a-tat-tat—

A portable tape recorder, plugged into a wall socket, sat on a stand near the window. With the aid of a tuner/amplifier and dual hi-fi speakers it provided all the sound. The electronic ghost of Walter Zink.

"Jay-jay!"

He whipped around.

Carla, hands on hips, high color in her cheeks, glared at him. "You—you sneak!"

"Carla! I knocked, rang the bell, hollered, but—"

"So now you know," she said. "He isn't here."

"I don't give a hoot where your father is. You're the one I'm looking for."

"Well, here I am," she said, somewhat mollified. "I heard you clear out in back. Thought you were a sub-poena server."

"A what?" In the room the tape tapped on. "For Pete's sake, Carla, go turn that thing off."

Carla vanished around the side of the house. Moments later the sound of typing ceased. Emerging from the front door, she sat down cross-legged on the grass and covered her face with her hands. "It's so hideously embarrassing," she said.

Jay-jay touched her on the shoulder. "I listen pretty good," he said. "If you need a friendly ear."

"Promise not to tell anybody?"

"My lips are sealed."

Carla peeked up at him between her fingers. "Daddy's hiding."

"Hiding?" Jay-jay had a momentary vision of that portly bearded author, Walter Zink, skulking about the farm at night, scrounging food, and hiding in the brush by day. Was *he* the Creep? Not hardly.

Carla nodded. "From his third wife. And her lawyers.

A dreadful woman. She's suing him for back alimony."

"Not your mother?"

"Mom died when I was a baby. This—harpy divorced Daddy last year. Ever since, she's been hounding him for money. That's why we're so poor. He can't pay her till he finishes his next book. So, to get shut of all the court orders and gook, he took off."

"And left you behind?"

"For a while. He had this neat idea, an endless loop tape. Repeats every six minutes, to scare off burglars and muggers and whatnot. When they hear it playing they'll believe somebody's home and go 'way."

"It fooled me," Jay-jay admitted. "But I fool easy. Where is he, do you know?"

"I don't," she said. "So I can't tell any legal beagle."

He listened to the faint pop of make-believe gunfire drifting from Camp P, a reminder of his mission. Was Peking Man make-believe too, like Operation Slasher and Daddy's "typewriter"? It seemed impossible that there could be any danger around here. But Comrade Chen was real. "Has anybody asked you about those bones?" he said.

Carla uncovered her face and eyed him quizzically. "Old Bubble Belly, your sergeant sidekick?"

"Not him," Jay-jay said and recounted the latest developments at the Flea Farm. All of them. Except one: the fate of the bones in Hattie's pulverizer. That, in the name of family pride or something like it, had to remain Hattie's secret.

Carla jumped to her feet, her eyes now wide and bright. "Wow! Half a million dollars?"

"That's how I heard it."

"We're partners in this, aren't we, Jay-jay? Share and share alike? You wouldn't have found them except for me."

"Sometimes I wish we hadn't found anything," he said. "But sure. Fifty-fifty."

"Wonderful! That solves everything. Daddy can pay his alimony, you can pay your taxes, Hattie can buy a new vat and—"

"Dream on," Jay-jay said. "Listen. You hear that?"

Carla tilted her head, then said in a small voice. "Oh. They're at it again."

He nodded. "War games. Along the creek. We can't go back till who knows when."

"So we wait," she said. "They can't last forever."

"Don't hold your breath."

"Pessimist," she said. "Do you think Creep stole our bones?"

Ensnared in his lie once again, Jay-jay said, "Must've. To chew on. I have a crazy mixed-up feeling about this dude. He's—uncivilized."

"Why don't you catch him?"

"I'm working on it. But he always seems two jumps ahead. Maybe three or four," Jay-jay said. Creep might be harmless as a puppy, Dr. Chen a nosey old fusspot, but Jay-jay felt responsible. Somebody had to look out for Walter Zink's one and only. "If any stranger comes around, grab the phone and ring me."

"Will do." She gave him a dazzling smile. "And, Jay-jay, thanks."

"For what?"

"For listening to my tale of woe. And not laughing."

"What's to laugh?" he said. "Keep in touch."

He was a few strides up the road when the tape began again. But this time it seemed to be repeating "half a million . . . half a million . . ."

# NINE

AFTER SUPPER THAT evening Jay-jay, at Hattie's bidding, moved her potting table across the garden and placed it near the tool shed. When he had scrubbed off the top Hattie laid out an assortment of fresh vegetables, a bowl of mixed salad greens, and a plate of cookies. Beside the table she put a kitchen chair.

"We want to make our friend feel at home," she said. "Welcome."

"He needs an invitation?" Jay-jay said. "Like, *Guess Who's Coming to Dinner?*"

Hattie sampled a cookie. "Everybody has a sweet tooth," she said. "I'm sure he'll come. If not tonight, then soon."

"Dressed how? In his birthday suit? Aunt Hattie, this Creep is something else."

"Jay-jay, he needs help and understanding. I feel it in my bones."

Jay-jay winced. Lately he'd become sensitive to that word.

"Also," she said, "I don't think we should refer to him as Creep. It's demeaning."

"What are you going to call him if he does turn up? *Mister* Creep?"

"That's not funny, Jay-jay. Be charitable."

No, not funny at all. But weird. Weird as the Mad Hatter's Tea Party. So why am I going along with this? Jay-jay asked himself. Because I love Aunt Hattie. "Maybe we should leave a pitcher of water," he said. "Our boy's so thirsty he's been drinking out of the creek."

"Poor lorn thing. I hope he won't take fright and bolt off again. Or trip over your alarm."

"A little gremlin tells me," Jay-jay said, "that he's doped it out already. But if your heart's set on this, I'm game. Just once."

Shortly before dark he carried Hattie's rocker from the house and placed it in the shed, near the door, where she could look out through a crack at the table and observe what, if anything, went on. Armed with flashlight and hand bell, Hattie settled into the chair with her knitting. Despite his skepticism, Jay-jay had to admit that her plan was simple to the point of genius. But was Creep hungry enough to cooperate?

"Aunt Hattie," he said, "if he takes one step toward you, ring your bell like crazy. Don't take any chances."

Hattie gathered up her yarn and needles. "Don't fret so, dear. I'll get a nice start on my afghan while I'm waiting."

With some misgivings Jay-jay left her and climbed to his room. The shed was only fifty yards away. In case of trouble he could react fast. But how fast was Creep? How smart was Creep? How strong? So far it had been demoralizing. No contest. Creep had won every match hands down.

Jay-jay stretched out on his bed, tossed and turned, then drifted into a restless sleep. When the alarm clock muffled under his pillow woke him at midnight, Jay-jay punched it off and slipped back to the tool shed. Hattie, still calmly knitting, whispered that all was quiet and went off to her own bed, leaving Jay-jay to man the watch till daybreak.

He slumped into the rocker and struggled to keep awake, to focus on the table outside in the starlight. Once he heard the distant, barely audible trill of a whistle, followed by more faint gunfire. Operation Slasher. Day and night. Night and day. Around the clock.

Jay-jay sighed and turned his thoughts to the more alluring topic of money. As Carla had pointed out, the reward would pay a lot of taxes. And in the process he'd be performing a service for the Chinese people. Dowser's good deed of the century. If he could pull it off.

The hours dragged by interminably. His conviction grew: This was not only a deadly bore but a waste of time. Creep wasn't coming tonight, feast or fast. Jay-jay toyed with the idea of venturing out to watch from a better vantage point, maybe stir up some action. But no. A promise was a promise. He sat and rocked and stared.

With the first pale hint of dawn Jay-jay gave up, stretched his cramped muscles, and left the shed. Nothing on the table had been touched. Aunt Hattie's sugar had caught no fly. But why, after four night visits in a row, had Creep been a no-show?

Because, Jay-jay had the chilling thought, the little devil knows this is a stakeout, a trap. Like he knows about my burglar alarm. Like he seems to know every move we make around here. Creep, the all-seeing ever-present Eye.

When he woke up in midmorning, grainy-eyed and sticky, Jay-jay sensed a major change in the weather. The wind had shifted halfway around the compass. It blew not off the Pacific, but over the mountains from the distant desert, a withering gust of air that sent thermometers soaring. A Santa Ana. Fire weather. Scorched earth weather.

Aunt Hattie was watering the garden. Quickly Jay-jay fell into the routine, coupling extra lengths of hose together, laying out soakers, scraping open new irrigation channels, wetting down beds of tender young plants. When a Santa Ana swooped down it often lasted for days. For farmers it was a bugle call to arms.

So much for the Weather Bureau and official forecasts. Nobody's perfect, he thought, not even Hattie.

About noon the mailman in his van made his daily stop out front, waved and drove on. Strolling to the box, Jay-jay pulled out the contents: a couple of bills, a seed catalogue, and a plain white envelope with his last name typed on the front.

"Dear Dowser," he read the enclosed typewritten note. "Please meet me at the Granada Reservoir at twelve o'clock today to discuss your reward. Come alone and do not tell anyone." It was signed in pen, "Chen."

He inspected the envelope again. No return address, no stamp. If it hadn't been delivered by regular mail, then how? By whom? How long ago? Had Chen himself or his bodyguard driven by and stuffed it in the box? Odd, but maybe that's how the comrades did business.

*Reward!* That was the key, the magic word. Maybe, Jay-jay thought wishfully, Chen is ready to pay something in advance, a sweetener to seal the deal.

He told Hattie he had to run an errand, promised to be

back shortly, and backed out the truck. On the road he turned left and drove up the hill. Half a mile beyond the last house he swung onto a one-lane road that climbed still deeper into the foothills, up a steep narrow grade into the southern California of yesteryear, B.B. Before the Boom. Before the subdividers and the land-hungry hordes. Before the smog. All that would come here too, someday, but today there was only space and quiet and clear blue sky and, finally, the old reservoir.

Abandoned years ago, it lay in a hollow ringed by dying eucalyptus trees and biscuit-colored boulders. Time and weather had eroded most of the earth-fill dam, leaving a dry bottom overgrown with brush. A lone cement-block shed had survived the creeping ruin. The place had an air of melancholy, of faded hopes and forgotten dreams.

Jay-jay parked the pickup and gazed about. Nobody in sight. No car. He checked his watch. Twelve-fifteen. Surely Chen would have waited a quarter of an hour. So Chen must be late too.

He walked over to the shed, a squat windowless bunker that had been a powder magazine when the dam was under construction. The rusty bolt yielded to his yank. He pulled open the metal door on squealing hinges and peered inside. Nothing but dust and the stench of ages. A generation of kids had scratched their graffiti on the walls. Overhead, the papery rustle of dead leaves in the wind intensified the silence.

At the sound of an approaching motor Jay-jay turned, his eyes on the road.

A red station wagon topped the rise and braked beside his truck. Two men got out, one large, the second larger. Strangers, white, anyway not Chinese, dressed alike in suntans and billed baseball caps, both in sun glasses. Suddenly Jay-jay felt uneasy.

*You can't trust a Commie. . . . Tell him to drop dead. . . . Take care, kid.* Words of counsel from Master Sergeant Moose Majeski. "You fellows looking for me?" he called.

"If your name's Dowser." The first man stepped forward and stuck out his hand. "I'm Smith. He's Jones."

Jay-jay shook and bobbed his head at Number Two. "Mr. Smith. Mr. Jones. Where's Dr. Chen?"

"Called away at the last minute," Smith said. "We work for him."

Jay-jay looked from one man to the other, then over at their wagon, and wet his lips. The Santa Ana heat seemed suffocating, like a noose around his neck, choking off his air. Something wrongo about this pair, he realized now. They hadn't met him by appointment. They must've been waiting down below, watching, out of sight, then followed him to the reservoir. To make sure I took the bait. And did I ever! Hook, line, and sinker.

"Chen sent us about the reward money," Smith said. And to his pal, "Right, Jonesy?"

Jonesy, now standing alongside Smith in a solid wall of flesh, said, "Ri-i-i-ight."

"Money." Jay-jay gave a feeble laugh. "I sure can use some."

Smith laughed too, but louder. "Can't we all? But first we want to see the goods, or a sample."

"Goods?"

"Bones," Smith said. "Peking Man." He pronounced it "Peekin'."

"I don't have any bones," Jay-jay said. "Not one."

"But you know where they are."

Jay-jay tried to read Smith's eyes behind the shades. Play it cool, Dowser. Do you try for the truck? Do you run for it, take to the brush on foot? The nearest house and help is miles away. Nobody knows where you are. You're out here in the Great Big Lonesome, on your own. He said, "Dr. Chen told me no third parties. Do you have any identification?"

"Don't you trust us, Dowser?" Smith said. "Chen has a real mean temper when he's crossed. Right Jonesy?"

"Ri-i-i-ight."

"I'm not crossing anybody," Jay-jay said. "But the bones, they're on the base. Pennington. Hard to get at."

"You just tell us whereabouts on Pennington. We'll get at 'em."

"Well, I don't know exactly—" Jonesy, the bigger man, looked to be the slower, not too bright. But he had moved in closer, almost pinning Jay-jay against the hut. "They're in a restricted area. Closed to civilians. You're not Marines, are you, fellows?"

"Come off it, buster," Smith said. "We want the Peekin' Man."

"You'll need a pass," Jay-jay said, improvising wildly. When in trouble send for the Marines. The only Marine I know is Moose Majeski. Help me, Moose, Help!

"So we get a pass," Smith said. "Pass to where?"

Jay-jay sucked in a breath that seared like flame. "Go see Sergeant Majeski. Ask him. He can tell you."

"Moose Majeski? Old Satchel Mouth?" Smith exchanged a look with Jonesy. "Could be, though. He's got his hand in everybody's pocket. How'd he rope a kid like you into this, Dowser?"

"We're partners, sort of. He—he knows where the bones are buried. Only one who does."

Smith frowned. "What's this partner crud? If you're lying—"

"Me? Lie?" Jay-jay dredged up a sickly smile. "To you? To Dr. Chen? Do I look that dumb?"

Smith stared at him a moment, then said, "No, I guess you don't. Take him, Jonesy."

Jay-jay broke for the gap between them, but the slow dumb-looking Jonesy feinted left and shifted right faster than a cheetah. Pain exploded inside Jay-jay's skull and the flame engulfed him.

Jay-jay rolled over on his back, opened one eye, and stared up through a canopy of leaves at blue sky. Reassured by this familiar sight, he tried to stand but his legs betrayed him. His stomach heaved, his head throbbed, his mouth tasted like a chem lab. He explored his teeth with a furry tongue and decided he'd been doped with knockout drops.

His watch read five o'clock. He'd been lying here for hours. Groggily he reconstructed the events, arranging them in sequence. First the note from Dr. Chen. The drive up the hill to the reservoir. Smith and Jones. Then—KAPOW! He groaned and got to his knees and finally to his feet and leaned against a eucalyptus for support.

The Santa Ana wind had died down but the air still felt furnace hot. He had to get back and help Hattie with the watering. By now she must be worried.

Jay-jay discovered the contents of his pockets strewn under the tree. Evidently Chen's gorillas had dragged him back in the brush, searched him, and then split for Pennington. But what had they been after? A single name? And why had they drugged him? To buy more time, so that he couldn't warn Majeski? But that didn't make much sense; Chen already knew about Majeski.

Too dizzy to think, he stumbled up the rise to his truck and crawled in. A punch on the starter button produced a whirring noise. He got out again, lifted the hood, and pulled up the distributor cap. Smith and Jones had removed the rotor, leaving him grounded.

At that black moment Jay-jay's heart's desire was to sack out under the nearest tree and sleep, sleep, sleep. Maybe some fairy godmother would happen along and rescue him. Nobody else was likely to, not during a Santa Ana. Or he could walk home. But in his condition that might take till Christmas.

No rotor spare, he thought, but I still have wheels. Remember the law of gravity, Dowser. Gravity holds the universe together. What goes up must come down, including one truck and an idiot driver.

Jay-jay surveyed the turnaround area. Small, not much room to maneuver, but almost level. Unfortunately, with no concern for the future, he had parked hind-end to, pointed toward the reservoir. Which left only one way to go—a one-hundred-eighty-degree turn on sheer muscle power.

He released the hand brake, slid the gear lever into neutral, cramped the front wheels, then limped around to the rear, leaned his shoulder against the tailgate, and shoved. With all the strength of a baby chickadee. The truck rolled a few inches, stopped, and rolled back to its original position.

In his frustration Jay-jay felt like bawling, shedding

tears for himself. The temperature must be over a hundred degrees. How long since he'd had a drink? Now if I were Creep, he thought, I'd dig a hole somewhere and find water. But I'm not Creep. I'm me.

Move it, man!

Searching, he found a large flattish rock and wedged it behind the left rear tire. He braced his feet, straightened the kink out of his back, and attacked the tailgate once more. This time the truck gained a foot. He toed the rock forward to block the roll back. Progress, a little.

Jay-jay rested a minute, caught his breath, then pushed off. Another foot, maybe more, and block again. Rest, repeat, then block, over and over again until the blood was roaring in his ears and his stomach churned with dry heaves. Easy now, he warned himself; don't blank out. You could tip this heap right over the bank into the reservoir.

The sun was a low fiery ball by the time he had the Ford turned around, pointed toward the road. A road-runner—rare sight these days—startled him, zipping across the dam site like a feathered rocket. Jay-jay stiffened, listening intently. A car grinding up the grade? No. Only the wind again, a sultry evening breeze.

He opened the door on the driver's side and gave a final running shove. As the truck gathered speed he leaped inside. In the rear view mirror he caught one last glimpse of Granada Reservoir and then the road rushed at him. If these brakes burn out, he thought, I'll end up in the Pacific Ocean. If I meet somebody coming up, head on—

The pickup plunged downhill, bouncing over ruts and rocks, careening around sharp bends. Tools rattled and banged. Dust billowed behind. Brush whizzed past in a blur. Jay-jay clung to the wheel so hard it felt imbedded in his palms.

On the steepest grades he braked, but sparingly, fearful of losing momentum for the one climb ahead. Then suddenly he was on it, a long straight pitch that looked higher than Mount Everest. Up, up, up, creeping now, wheels slowing, almost to a standstill. Jay-jay hammered his fist on the dash.

"Come on! You can do it! You gotta do it!"

And then, just barely, he nosed over the crest and rolled down the other side through diminishing foothills onto the main road.

Five minutes later he coasted to a stop in the farm driveway. Home sweet home, a haven from the slings and arrows of outrageous fortune. Weak with relief and wet with sweat, he slumped back and then blinked. A gleaming dark sedan was parked there. Beside it stood a large man in a black suit and chauffeur's cap. An Asian.

It took Jay-jay's spinning brain a moment to make the connection. Chen's bodyguard! Chen, the comrade doctor from Peking, here? Now? In Aunt Hattie's yard? Or worse, inside the house?

Some days it didn't pay to get out of bed.

# TEN

THE BODYGUARD STOOD motionless, impassive. Jay-jay stared at what appeared to be a bulge under the man's left armpit. A gun? Or muscle? It really didn't matter at this point, he told himself fatalistically. He'd reached rock bottom, end of the line for a downhill racer.

He opened the door, stepped out, and said, "Where's your boss?"

The guard lifted one shoulder in a universal gesture that said, I don't speak your language.

Jay-jay walked past him, rounded the corner of the house, and stopped. Aunt Hattie had placed a folding card table under the pepper tree and set it with a snowy cloth, silverware, and china. At the moment she was filling a cup from a porcelain pot and saying to her guest, "Do have another cookie, Doctor. They're nonfattening."

Dr. Chen, his back to Jay-jay, reached for a plate and replied, "Delicious, Miss Gribben. You must give me your recipe."

"That nephew of mine," Hattie bubbled on. "I don't know what's keeping him. Young people nowadays are so—" Catching sight of Jay-jay, she broke off.

Chen turned, rose from his chair, and gave a starchy little bow. "Ah, Mr. Dowser," he said. "A privilege to meet you once again."

"Your friend stopped by to call and introduced himself," Hattie explained. "You're just in time to join us, Jay-jay dear. We're having tea."

"And," Chen added, "a most interesting conversation."

Bug-eyed, Jay-jay mumbled, "Conversation? That's nice."

"Dr. Chen is a gardener too," Hattie said. "He raises flowers. In Peking, China."

"Nice," Jay-jay repeated idiotically. "Very nice."

"In a small way," Chen said. "Purely for pleasure. Most Chinese are close to the soil, to Mother Earth."

"Dr. Chen uses a mulch of mulberry leaves," Hattie went on. "We'll have to try that sometime, Jay-jay. I was telling him about our bone meal."

Jay-jay paled. Had Hattie, in her innocence, spilled the beans? Was that why Chen had returned, to pump his aunt for information? "Uh—oh—bone meal," he stammered. "Old cow bones, you know. We buy it at the store. In fifty-pound sacks."

Chen smiled. "In China we raise few cows. More water buffalo. But I presume buffalo bones would serve the purpose." He turned back to Hattie and bowed again. "It has been delightful, Miss Gribben. But duty calls. If you'll excuse us now, I'd like a word with your nephew."

"Ta-ta, doctor," she chirped. "Next time stay for supper."

In a state of shock Jay-jay followed Chen to his car. No longer smiling, Chen spoke a few sharp words to the bodyguard, then switched back to English. "Mr. Dowser," he said, "I trust you've had time to digest my report. Have you reached a decision?"

Jay-jay looked around the yard and over at the trees. No sign of Smith and Jones or their wagon. But they could be somewhere near, waiting, hidden. By now, he assumed, they had located Moose Majeski and learned the truth. Which was that Jay-jay had lied to save his precious neck. He fished the note from his pocket and handed it over without a word.

Chen settled his glasses on his nose, studied the note and then the envelope. Finally he emitted a sound somewhere between a sniff and a snort. "A forgery," he said. "A fraud. A clumsy one. Explain please."

Jay-jay did, from beginning to end. "They claimed they work for you," he said. "Who are they?"

"Hah! Smith and Jones. Obviously hirelings of the running-dog lackeys of Taiwan."

"Running-dog which?"

"The so-called government of Nationalist China," Chen said. "The fools who lost the bones in the first place."

"You just lost *me*," Jay-jay said. "You mean Taiwan—"

"Precisely," Chen said. "Bandits. Criminals. Hooligans. They too want Peking Man. Their agents will stop at nothing."

"Can't you stop them?"

"Oh yes. There is one sure way." Chen's lips twitched. "Turn over the remains to me. Very simple. Smith, Jones, and company will then lose interest in you. Completely."

"But I—"

"But you still maintain your masquerade of ignorance," Chen interrupted. "No, please, my dear Mr. Dowser. Do not try to deceive me. You are most transparent."

Jay-jay glanced at the bodyguard, who looked about as transparent as a slab of beef. Mouse-trapped, he thought. Damned if I do and damned if I don't. Whose side is Chen really on? "I need more time," he said.

"Time for what?"

"For—for something to happen."

"And how soon will that be?"

"Depends," Jay-jay said. "If you get the bones how soon do I get the money?"

"First things first," Chen said. "Then we will discuss your reward. And, Mr. Dowser—"

"Yes?"

"A word of caution. Do not dawdle or delay. Time, like death, waits on no man. Your good health, young sir."

With that Chen was gone, into his limousine, and soon whizzing down the road.

Jay-jay stared at the settling dust. Well, time might not wait, but he, young sir, had to wait on General What's-His-Name. On Operation Slasher. Meanwhile, had Dr. Chen hired Smith and Jones to rough him up, to scare him into action? For the answer, don't miss next week's program.

Hattie was clearing the table when he returned to the yard. "Such a charming gentleman," she said. "And, Jay-jay, another friend phoned this morning, just after you left. Mr. Leo."

"Mr. Leo?"

"Leo the lion, silly. The big one with the jailhouse haircut."

"Oh," Jay-jay said. "Moose. What did he want?"

"He said he was leaving for the weekend. Not to call him." Hattie scrabbled in her apron pocket and withdrew a scratch pad. "He said to give you this message: 'The deal is off Sunday.' Whatever that means."

Good question, Jay-jay thought wearily. He had no deals upcoming with Majeski Sunday or any other day. Just his own survival.

But the first part of the message rang through. If Moose had left Camp P for the weekend he hadn't been there when Smith and Jones, those running-dog lackeys of Taiwan—or of Peking—had shown up with their questionnaire. Maybe they would give up now, go away, fade into the sunset.

Do you believe that, Dowser? Sure. You and the guy who bought the Brooklyn Bridge. "Aunt Hattie," he said, "I'm bushed. Long day. Can you finish the watering?"

"You trot along, dear." She blew him a kiss. "I'll hook up the sprinkler."

Jay-jay tottered to the tower and climbed to his room, feeling like a tackle dummy. As for today's performance, he *was* a dummy, a real nerd. For a moment he lingered at the window, face to the Santa Ana. Tomorrow would be another stinger.

Down below, Hattie was resetting the table with a pitcher of water and a salad bowl. For Creep, minus silverware and china. Would Creep come back tonight or had he left for good? Jay-jay smiled as he snuggled into bed. He was almost beginning to miss the little cuss.

. . .

KER-THUNK. Jay-jay awoke with a start and sat up, eyes open in the darkness of his room. Lordy, lordy, he thought, it's hotter than ever. That Santa Ana is one killer. I must've been dreaming.

KER-THUNK. It came again, an unmistakable thud against the tower siding.

He groped for the light switch and stopped, his mind racing. The other time this had happened—it seemed years ago—he'd caught Chen snooping. Was the doctor back for a replay? Or those two goons?

Jay-jay stared out his west window into the yard and garden, the 'cado grove, the oaks, and brushy thickets beyond. A fat moon cast its waxen light but he saw no movement, heard no sound. Even the Marines on maneuvers at Camp P two miles away seemed dead to the world. There was only the night and the softly pulsing desert wind.

"Creep," he whispered, "you threw those rocks. You did! I know you did. Then went and hid. Are you trying to tell me something?"

He fumbled behind the clothes rack and hauled out a baseball bat, the one he'd saved from Pony League the time he'd hit his first and only homer. Hefting it in one fist, he scaled down the ladder and crouched in shadow, all his aches and pains forgotten. A minute passed. False alarm? he wondered. Creep playing some prank to prove how sharp he was, and Jay-jay wasn't? Fun an' games?

Over by Las Pulgas Creek a motor started up. It had to be on the side road, Jay-jay knew, the one that dead-ended at Pennington, but trees screened it from his view. The car was moving slowly now, without lights, the engine making a pussycat purr. It turned onto the main road and the headlights flashed on. The driver accelerated and took off, heading south toward town at a fast clip.

Jay-jay squeezed the bat handle in frustration. He hadn't caught a glimpse of car or driver. Something must have frightened him—or them—away. Or maybe "they" had finished whatever "they" had come here to do. Which, for half a million dollars, might be almost anything.

Suddenly he tensed. An acrid smell of smoke drifted to him on the breeze.

On his side of the creek, opposite the road, a yellow curl of light blossomed. Fanned by the wind, it sprang into flame. Jay-jay stared in horror. Fire! In this weather a fire could be disaster, a blitzkrieg. He'd seen them before in other places, brush fires that wiped out whole hillsides in minutes. Fences. Barns. Houses. And sometimes people.

He ran to the house, shouting at his aunt's bedroom window. "Hattie, wake up! Fire!"

No response. Aunt Hattie once had slept through an earthquake, four-point-nine on the Richter scale. He pounded on the frame and bellowed, "Call the fire department! Hurry!"

Her bedside lamp snapped on at last.

Jay-jay sprinted across the garden, one eye on the spreading crimson glow at the far end. Too late he remembered his burglar alarm. Tripped by the wire, he sprawled face down among some cauliflower. Cowbells rattled and clanked, a raucous clamor that shattered the night.

Oh great! he thought as he sat up giddily and rubbed a

smarting shin. Burglars, beware. This joint is wired for sound. Dowser's foolproof anti-crime invention, patent pending.

He stumbled to his feet, limped to the shed and grabbed a spare coil of hose. This he attached to the nearest faucet, coupled it with a second hose and that to a third. All thumbs and fumbling fingers, he then removed the sprinkler head and screwed on a nozzle. Seconds counted now. The fire already had an awesome headstart.

He spun open the valve, praying for a full head of pressure, and hauled out his line to the limit. It reached, barely. Flames crackled and sizzled through the powder-dry brush, embers popped, and smoke rose in choking swirls. Another three minutes, he told himself, and this'll be a monster out of control. Unless I can slow it down—

Playing his stream of water from side to side across a ten-yard front, Jay-jay retreated one step at a time as the fire advanced. Licking tongues of flame died, then leaped again with renewed fury. Ashes hissed, steam mingled with the smoke in a dense cloud, fiery particles quivered in the superheated air like angry wasps.

Touch and go, he thought. Go as in *goner*. Hose down the right flank, then the left, and back off another step. Where's the fire crew? Down the road five long miles. Or out fighting another fire. Sweet Santa Ana.

Then Aunt Hattie popped up beside him, slicker thrown over her nightgown, her feet in woolly slippers. She threw down a shovel and a machete, pulled the hose away from him, and took over.

"You call the firehouse?" he gasped.

"On their way," she said. "Hop to it, boy!"

With Hattie on the hose and Jay-jay alternately chopping brush and shoveling dirt, they fought side by side. Fought and gradually tamed the beast. The blaze crept forward a few more yards, wavered and fell back, feeding on itself, finally soaked and smothered into submission except for a hot spot or two.

In the distance Jay-jay heard the howl of a siren. He blinked his streaming eyes, wiped the soot off his face, and uttered a feeble "Whew-ee!"

"We could have been burned out," Hattie said. "Lock, stock, and barrel. Lucky you woke up when you did."

"No luck to it," he said. "Creep woke me."

"Are you sure?" she asked.

"Ninety-nine percent. That's twice now."

Hattie peered over her shoulder. "I just don't understand why he's such a shrinking violet."

"He may be shy but he's some night watchman." Jay-jay leaned on his shovel and gazed at the sodden smoldering mess. "Seems like we can use one lately."

A county pumper truck arrived shortly and half a dozen black-clad firemen piled off to finish the job professionally. Jay-jay, hero of the hour, was detained at the scene by a chief who had some questions to ask. Sheriff's deputy Hoyle, who arrived separately in his blue-domed cruiser, stood by, an attentive witness to the interview.

Chief: Now, son, you did a fine job, considering the wind and all. Might've been a bearcat. Kept your wits. But let me get this straight. You think somebody set the fire? On purpose?

Jay-jay: Yes, sir.

Chief: Couldn't have been some careless driver who tossed out a live butt?

Jay-jay: No, sir. This guy was parked over there.

Maybe more than one. All of a sudden he took off. No lights at first. When he hit the road he punched it.

Chief: Hmmm. Funny place to park. You see this person?

Jay-jay: No. It was moonlight, but those oak trees—

Chief: You get a make on the car?

Jay-jay: No.

Chief: Just the sound, huh? You have any idea who might pull a stunt like this? It's arson, a serious charge. Some sorehead, a nut?

Jay-jay: Nobody I can think of at the moment.

Chief: Well, keep thinking, son. We'll check it out.

Jay-jay: Thank you, sir.

After the chief and his crew departed Deputy Hoyle, still waiting in the wings, stepped forward. "Hello, Jay-jay," he said. "Remember me?"

Jay-jay sighed. After the last day and night he could hardly remember his own name. The stench of charred brush and chemical foam seemed to fog his brain. "Sure do," he said. "Is this your regular beat?"

"Oh, I cover all bases," Hoyle said. "Or try to. I got to wondering if you'd seen that creep again, the long-haired nature boy."

Jay-jay flexed one hand. He had blisters on both sides. From the shovel on his palm, from sparks on the back. His hair smelled singed "I never did see him," he said. "You still looking, Mr. Hoyle?"

"We got just that one complaint." Hoyle hitched at his belt and sagging holster. "But in my line of work, Jay-jay, we don't like loose ends. It occurred to me he might be hanging around the area."

"Around here? Why?"

The deputy smiled. "What we call the long arm of co-incidence. Take your fire tonight. We can't pin it on your neighbor Tuffy, can we? Tuffy's in Hawaii with his folks. So, who done it?"

"You believe it was the Creep?"

"In cases like this," Hoyle said, "we look for a disturbed personality. Somebody with a screw loose, a kink in his head. Maybe plays with matches. How many firebugs do you have in one neighborhood?"

"But he doesn't—" Jay-jay broke off. Who doesn't what, Dowser? Creep *doesn't play with matches.* But how could you possibly know that? What he did do, he saved your bacon tonight, maybe saved the whole farm. You can't throw him to the wolves, not now.

"You were saying," Hoyle prompted.

"Why, uh, I'll sure keep watching for him," Jay-jay said. Half a truth was better than none.

"You do that." The deputy gave him a long close look. "G'night." And drove away.

Jay-jay watched the deputy's taillights disappear down the road. Had Hoyle believed him? Maybe. But I'm a lousy liar, he thought, and a worse actor. I covered for you this once, Creep. But that deputy, he'll be back. What do I tell him next time?

# ELEVEN

"JAY-JAY, YOO-HOO!"

He sat up in bed, stretching and yawning, feeling a twinge of guilt that he had slept so late, almost till noon. The hot lifeless air told him the Santa Ana hadn't gone away. Nor had his troubles. How nice it would be, he thought, to pull the sheet over his head, say to heck with all the world and zonk out again.

"Company here," Hattie called. "Stir your stumps, boy."

Jay-jay put on a clean shirt and pants and stepped to the door in time to see his aunt disappear inside the house. Carla Zink stood in the garden below, peering up. "Sorry to wake you," she said. "But this is important."

"Let me guess," he said. "Your Daddy's back?"

Carla made a face at him. "May I come up? I've never seen your pad." He nodded and she climbed the ladder. Poised in the doorway, she gazed about his room and said, " 'S' wonderful. Like a tree house."

Pleased, Jay-jay said, "Cool in summer, snug in winter. Everything but inside plumbing."

"Can't you pipe in water from that tank on top?"

"Empty," he said. "Has been for years. Except for mice."

"What's underneath?"

"Storage space. Old furniture. Hardware. Junk." A breeze stirred, bearing the smell of charred wood. "You know about the fire last night?"

"Your aunt told me. It's scary," Carla said. "That's why I'm here. Stick your head outside and listen."

Jay-jay did. A blanket of silence lay over the land, which seemed to shimmer under layers of heat. "I don't hear anything."

"Natch," she said. "The Marines called off their war games. Till further notice. Because of the fire hazard."

"That doesn't sound like General Whiz Bang," Jay-jay said.

"He did, though. Orders from headquarters. I phoned Information Center on Camp P and got the word. Official."

Jay-jay recalled the cryptic message Moose Majeski had left with Hattie yesterday: *The deal is off Sunday.* Which meant, he realized now, that Operation Slasher had been shut down temporarily. To the Moose everything was a "deal." It might get back on the track tomorrow, if the Santa Ana petered out.

"Remember the old proverb: It's an ill wind that blows no man good." Carla regarded him with her level gaze. "Now's our chance. While this weather lasts."

"Now? Right now?"

"Why not? I bring you the best news ever, pure gold, and you act like a zombie."

"Because I'm weak from hunger," Jay-jay said. "No

breakfast. No supper last night. No lunch yesterday. I'm starved."

"Go eat then," she said. "While you're doing that I can read the report."

"What report?"

"The one you said the Chinese doctor gave you. About Peking Man."

"Dr. Chen." Jay-jay butted a palm against his forehead. "I'm really dim today." He got his laundry bag off the wall hook, emptied it on his bed, pawed through dirty socks and shirts until he uncovered the brown envelope, which he handed to Carla. A detail nagged at him. Holes in his socks? A hole in his head? Something missing? He counted the shirts twice and came up with the same number.

Carla glanced up from her reading. "What now?"

"Only two shirts here," he said. "Should be three."

"Who washes your clothes?" she asked. "Aunt Hattie?"

"I do. When I get around to it. I wore that shirt yesterday. Stuffed it in the bag last night."

"Jay-jay—" Carla put down the report and gave him an anxious glance. "Are you sure you feel all right?"

"Sure I'm sure," he said hotly. "I'm telling you, that shirt is gone."

"Jeepers, who would pinch one stinky shirt? What for?"

Don't argue with the lady, he told himself. She's worried about you. She cares. That's cool. But if you tell her what you think you're thinking now, she'll say you've flipped. "Must've counted wrong," he mumbled.

He hadn't, though. He knew he'd counted right. And the discrepancy buzzed inside his skull like a trapped fly.

An hour later, after demolishing a stack of hotcakes, he set out with Carla down the back road, on foot. The truck, a lifeless hulk without its rotor, sat where he'd left it the evening before. Carla carried the shovel and four empty bags, Jay-jay a canteen of water and his rucksack containing sandwiches, Carla's instant camera, and a flashlight. They were prepared, as she put it, for "all eventualities," daylight or dark.

The afternoon was a roaster, silent except for occasional flurries of wind. The gray dust-coated undergrowth on either side seemed almost menacing, tinder ready to explode, a holocaust waiting to happen. No wildlife stirred from cover. Even the birds were still. Gloomy Sunday.

At the end of the road they stopped to rest in the shade and reconnoiter. The clearing lay empty under a sun ringed by sulfur-yellow halos. Beyond the fence, Camp P—Jay-jay's battleground, Target X, scene of past failure and future hope—simmered in bake oven heat. He wiped his face, passed the canteen to Carla, and took a swig himself. "All quiet on the Western Front," he said. "But don't forget the MPs."

"How could I ever?" she said. "But do they patrol in daytime?"

"That's Dowser's law: Expect the worst and you won't be disappointed."

"Pearls of wisdom from the guru," Carla said. "Tell me, what's Dr. Chen like?"

"Inscrutable. Man of many faces." Jay-jay explained about the secret agents hired by Taiwan and his misadventure with Smith and Jones. The no-goodnicks who would stop at nothing. Bandits, according to Chen. "I don't know what to believe," Jay-jay said. "The two governments could be bidding against each other. And guess who's in the middle."

"Perfect," Carla said. "How can we lose?"

"In one easy lesson," He gripped her hand and pulled her to her feet.

They dropped down into the creek bottom and pushed on through the brush to the culvert. The memory of Moose Majeski's backward exit from same brightened Jay-jay's day briefly. He crawled in, squirmed along under the fence, emerged on the far side, and helped Carla scramble up the bank.

This part of the clearing was pitted with shallow holes, flanked by mounds of dirt, as though an army of prairie dogs had been interrupted in their excavations. Foxholes. One-holers, two-holers, and some that looked too small for midgets.

"I wonder how many the general dug," Carla said.

"Can you imagine old Moose stuck in this one?" Jay-jay said. "He'd get his bee-hind shot off."

They stared about at the refuse of make-believe war: Cartridge casings, discarded ration cartons, empty ammo boxes. Scars gouged by tank treads and heavy artillery trucks. Operation Slasher had been cancelled in a hurry. The cleanup job, Jay-jay thought, would be one super headache but there were no casualties. Only pretend blood and wounds and bodies. Why can't we fight every war like this?

"I don't think I'd like to be a Marine," Carla said.

"There're worse careers," he said.

"Are you serious?"

"I guess I am," Jay-jay surprised himself by answering.

"Lived next door all these years and never thought about it before."

Picking their way among holes, they moved toward the jungle of chaparral and oaks that screened Las Pulgas here. Jay-jay halted at the edge to orient himself. The hut was invisible even in this direct harsh light. Perhaps the Marines had never stumbled across it or, if they had, left it undisturbed. The USMC had more on its collective mind than one deserted adobe shell.

Carla lowered her voice to a whisper. "I have that funny feeling again. Vibes."

"Me too," Jay-jay admitted. "But I don't know whether they're good or bad." Was it possible, he wondered, that hundreds of men could have skirmished here night and day without investigating every square inch of terrain? One encouraging sign: Litter ended where the brush began. Yes or no, he'd have his answer soon.

Carla grabbed his arm. "Pssst!"

He turned slowly but heard only the drowsy afternoon drone of insects. Bugville. Then a sound came to him, faint and indistinct—a voice.

He and Carla sank to their knees behind a clump of lemon berry. After a minute he allowed himself to hope. Maybe some kids playing beyond the fence. Or a couple out for a Sunday stroll. But presently two men walked into view on the far side of the clearing some distance away. *Inside* the fence. Both had on suntans, baseball caps, and sunglasses. Big men. One carried a roll of paper under his arm.

"MPs?" Carla whispered.

Jay-jay shook his head. "MPs would be in uniform."

The one with the paper unrolled it, knelt, placed it on

the ground and bent close. After a moment's inspection he raised his head and pointed.

On the shifting wind Jay-jay caught two words, "map . . . creek . . ." Suddenly his stomach tightened. The two sweetie pies who called themselves Smith and Jones, the same pair who had shanghaied him to the old reservoir the day before, who might have started the fire last night. What had Chen called them? *Running-dog lackeys of Taiwan.*

"What are they doing here?" Carla asked.

"Same thing we are," Jay-jay said. "I think. Hunting for bones."

The two men plodded across the clearing with a purposeful gait, skirting foxholes. Smith, the leader, and Jones, the stupid-looking lout with the dynamite moves. Watching their approach. Jay-jay realized that they hadn't spotted him and Carla. Not yet. They had not come through the culvert, but from the Pennington side, as bold as brass baboons. Could they be Marines?

"But how?" Carla whispered.

"Beats me," Jay-jay said. Clearly S and J knew something he didn't. But then, everybody seemed to know more. He was the latest of Johnny-come-latelies to this bash, the uninvited guest at the party, the kid who got no birthday cake. "Don't move and keep your head down."

"Maybe they're hunting for you," Carla said.

"Friendly they ain't," he said. "Now shush."

The two men stopped not far away. Smith consulted his map again, looked around, and said in a carrying voice, "This has gotta be the place. Matches the poop I heard in the NCO club. Regular jungle along the upper crick."

"Ri-i-i-ight," Jones agreed.

"We've been looking long enough, God knows," Smith said. "Tell you what, Jonesy. We'll start at the fence and work downstream. Together. Cover every bloody foot. Slow but sure."

"Ri-i-i-ight," said Jonesy and added a full sentence. "I sure hope the MPs don't drop on us."

"Screw them," Smith said. His black shades shifted back and forth over the brush like twin gun mounts. Then the crunch of footsteps receded toward the fence.

After a long silence Jay-jay raised his head. His heart was thudding and the sweat on his upper lip felt icy. *The poop I heard in the NCO club,* Smith had said. Did every noncom in the Corps know about Peking Man? And blab?

Carla tugged his sleeve. "They'll be coming back this way."

Jay-jay found his hand was shaking. He and Carla had to hide, but where? S and J had cut off the escape route to the rear. Maybe I can outrun them in a sprint, he thought, ditch them for a little while. Long enough for Carla to get free. If those apes find her—

"Jay-jay, hurry!"

His gaze fell on the glistening mounds of dirt, scattered at random like unfinished graves. One skill the USMC taught its recruits was how to dig under pressure. Graves galore. He had a sudden glimmer of an idea. "I'm gonna decoy them," he said. "Military diversion. You stay put. Don't bat an eyelash."

"You can't, Jay-jay. That's insane!"

"Watch me." He pulled off his rucksack, yanked out the flashlight. "Soon as they come blasting by, you take off. On the fly. For the culvert. Get out of here."

"And leave you behind with THEM?"

So who do you think you are? he asked himself. Sir Lancelot? St. George versus the Dragon? Butch Cassidy and Sundance on the late-late show, defying death and fate and stuff? Bub, you're a plastic hero, scared pink, and your knees are knocking. "Here goes," he said. "Gung-ho."

He slipped from behind the lemon berry, got a glimpse of Smith and Jones's retreating backs, then eased down to the bottom of the clearing, which ended in another tangle of head-high chaparral. He stopped, faced around and waited, the blood thrumming in his ears. Any moment now S and J would stop too, cut off by the fence, and swing around. And see him across the open, a long four hundred yards away. He'd make sure, double-dare sure, they did.

With a quick twist Jay-jay unscrewed the flashlight's base cap and shook out the batteries. A second twist at the front end released the lens, bulb, and reflector. Which left the casing, a hollow black cylinder about ten inches long and one inch in diameter. Useless for anything. Except that it might save him another beating, or worse.

At that second the two men reached the fence. They halted briefly, apparently discussing plans, their backs still to Jay-jay, then stepped toward the creek.

Jay-jay gulped air into his lungs and cupped his hands. "Hey, Smith!" he yelled. "Hey, Jones! Yanh, yanh, yanh!" He bounced up and down and thumbed his nose. "Ya bums!"

Jonesy was the first to react. He stiffened, half-turned, and shaded his eyes with one hand.

For good measure, and for Carla's benefit, Jay-jay

heaped jibe upon insult, an invitation to pursuit. "Yeah, it's me, Dowser. Come on, you slobs!"

Jonesy let out a roar and broke into full gallop, closely followed by his pal.

Jay-jay whirled and raced into the brush. Dodging, leaping, twisting, he plunged ahead. Branches swiped at his face, thorns raked his bare arms—enemies in wait to slow him. Once he tripped, sprawled headlong, got up and charged on. A world-class quarter-miler could cover the distance in forty-five seconds. S and J would take longer, what with confusion and delays. If he'd figured right he had a three-minute lead. No more and maybe less. Three minutes to get lost.

Feet dragging and chest heaving, he burst into the open again and skidded to a halt. A wide valley, no mere clearing, spread before him, bordered on his right by the timbered course of Las Pulgas. Operation Slasher had left its imprint everywhere. Foxholes and litter, holes and holes and more holes. He'd never seen so many. Far behind he heard a faint yammer. S and J hot on the scent. Human bloodhounds.

With a discriminating eye Jay-jay chose his hole. Not too deep and not too shallow, a narrow trench about six feet long, surrounded by other holes, some of which had caved in or been partially filled. He rolled in on his back and began to scoop frantically at the soft, loose sandy soil piled on either side.

It cascaded down in rivulets, covered his feet, his legs, his knees. He could hear nothing but his own scratchy breathing, think of nothing but one day long ago at the beach when he'd "buried" himself alive. For laughs. Up to his chin, a head without a body. You always were a show-off, he told himself. But this time you can't leave anything to show, not one lock of hair. Who's laughing now?

The dirt poured in on him, a weight that pressed down his lower body. It was harder to dig now, farther to reach. His fingertips felt raw, his arms ached. Slowly, ever so slowly, the cavity filled. His thighs, his belly, his chest disappeared under the brown flood. The silence grew oppressive. Surely Smith and Jones must be almost on top of him, closing in.

Buried to his neck, able to see only a wedge of sky directly above, he gulped one more deep breath, clamped the casing in his mouth, and shut his eyes tight. He felt a moment of terror when he clawed dirt over his face and head and patted it down, blotting out all light. Breath in, breathe out through his one-inch tube, his life support system, his air conditioner, his snorkel. He tamped more earth—hoping the flashlight case didn't stick up like a miniature stovepipe—wormholed his free hand underground and the job was done.

In his mind he composed an epitaph: *Here lies Julian Jerome Dowser, who departed this vale of tears mourned by all.* With a few exceptions.

Not for eternity, Jay-jay thought. Only for an hour or two or three. Until S and J got tired beating the bushes and went away. Far away. By now Carla also should be away. On the other side, the safe side, of Camp P's fence.

But how long was an hour? Or a minute? He counted to sixty several times. Too fast? Too slow? He lay rigid and tried to concentrate on the happy prospect of counting dollars. The numbers game. That, he discovered, could be boring, measured in units of either time or money. As a matter of fact, in his predicament, money seemed unreal, unimportant. The only reality was the air he inhaled and exhaled. Not to suffocate. Presently he became aware of a maddening itch under his nose. Unreachable. There was a muscle cramp in his left calf. Likewise. He felt a sneeze coming on. And he longed, desperately to burrow out a bit, poke his head up, and take a quick look. One tiny peek, then pop back down, no risk at all, hardly. He owed it to himself.

But suppose, Jay-jay thought, those two are up there now, watching close and waiting. Jones may be a klutz, but not Smith. Itch, cramp, sneeze, or whatever—no way, chum. Live with it. This just *seems* like forever. Dead is forever.

# TWELVE

By the time Jay-jay finally surfaced, twilight had crept over the land. With only his head and arms exposed he lay motionless, wondering if he had the strength to dig himself free. He spat out some mud, a filthy goo that had accumulated in his mouth, and ran his tongue over his teeth, wishing above all for a drink of water to wash away the awful yucky taste. He felt like a mummy, old King Tut, emerging from his sarcophagus after three thousand years.

Listening intently, Jay-jay could detect no unnatural sound. Doves cooed over among the sycamores. Somewhere a meadowlark warbled. Carefully he cleared away more dirt, sat up, and peered out at the empty valley. How much longer should he wait? Till dark? No, he decided. If S and J were still around they'd be combing the creek for bones, not hunting him. If.

The big "if" was whether or not Carla had escaped.

Dirt. He was a living clod, gritty and grainy. Dirt. In his nose, his ears, his hair, his pores. Brushing off the worst of it, Jay-jay squirmed out of the foxhole and made a cautious survey roundabout. The evening was calm and quiet, mellow in the soft honey light, and the air had changed. No longer dry and abrasive, it felt cool, fresh, out of the west. The Santa Ana was easing up. Tomorrow the Marines might be back, waging their shadow war.

He stuck the flashlight casing in his hip pocket, a reminder not to underestimate the enemy. Lose a few, win a few, but don't get careless. Smith and Jones could be anywhere.

Warily Jay-jay moved into the brush through which he'd come crashing hours before. Every few steps he paused to look around. Once he flushed a pair of quail who exploded under his feet with whirring wings and set his heart pounding. His strategy, once he gained the clearing, was to circle around it away from the creek, keeping to the undergrowth wherever possible. But to reach the culvert he would eventually have to cross open ground. That would be his moment of truth.

Had Smith and Jones found the hut by now? If so, and it seemed likely, he could kiss the reward goodbye. All that beautiful money. Another pipe dream down the tubes. But maybe he had distracted them, upset their plans and timing. Maybe. If you believed in miracles.

Ahead of him a twig snapped with a firecracker pop. Through the brush Jay-jay made out a motionless silhouette, the outline of a shoulder. Somebody had stopped not ten yards away, waiting and listening like himself. His breathing quickened. He tensed, ready to pivot and run.

Then Carla stepped into sight, carrying his rucksack, canteen, and shovel. When she saw him she gave a start and stared. He could have hugged her.

"Where have you been?" she demanded. "I was worried sick."

"Hiding," Jay-jay said. "Any water left?"

She handed him the canteen. He rinsed out his mouth and gulped down the longest sweetest drink in memory.

"Hiding where?" she said crossly. "Didn't you hear me calling?"

"In a hole with my ears plugged up."

Not quite believing, she looked him up and down, then her frown melted into a smile. "Some hole. You look like a coal miner."

Jay-jay wiped his face. "Camouflage," he said. "My disguise. What's with our boys?"

"Our boys," she said with relish, "got themselves collared by the MPs. Bye-bye. So long. *Adios.*"

"MPs? You saw them?"

She had indeed, Carla said. From beyond the fence, hiding behind a tree. An hour or so after Jay-jay performed his vanishing act, she explained, Smith and Jones had stomped back from their chase plainly in a foul and furious mood. They were arguing when two MPs in a helicopter surprised them in the clearing and landed.

"Could you hear what they said?" Jay-jay asked.

"I heard some new cuss words. Something about orders. Dangerous fire zone. Then the scene got wild."

"Wild how?"

One of the civilians—the one called Jonesy, she thought—had lost his temper and swung a fist at an MP. The MP swung back, with his billy club. The MP won. Jonesy and Smith had ended up in the chopper in handcuffs. "It was fun," Carla said. "Just like the movies."

"You bloodthirsty wench," Jay-jay laughed. "It couldn't happen to a nicer pair of fellas."

"You should be so lucky, my fine filthy friend." She handed him the shovel. "Let's go dig. Now. Before it's dark. Or the MPs or anybody else comes along."

They hurried up the rise and across the clearing, stopped to uncover the sacks that Carla had hidden under some leaves. Jay-jay had forgotten how thick the foliage was, nourished by underground moisture from the creek. Probably it never had been thinned or burned over since the days of the dons, when the Spanish ruled this land. Fire hazard? he thought. It's a ticking bomb. Which perhaps explained why there was no litter here: The Corps brass had ordered Las Pulgas strictly off limits, even to Operation Slasher.

Hold that happy thought, he told himself. You've had one near-miracle today. Now go for two.

In the lead, Carla pawed through more brush and pulled up beside an ancient oak. "I don't see it," she said. "Where's our hut?"

"Should have brought a compass," Jay-jay said. "Angle thataway."

"No, we're right on," she insisted. "I remember this old tree."

He rapped a knuckle against a massive gnarled trunk that could have been standing when the Pilgrims landed. Knock on wood, the money tree. "Our hut," he said, "is where we left it. Hasn't gone away."

"Okay, genius," Carla challenged. "You find it."

He stepped past her, peering right and left and straight ahead, sniffing decayed vegetation. This place looked the same, smelled the same, but something had changed. What? The light, that must be it. They'd come before at night. Did daylight make that much difference, distort his sense of direction, his judgment of distance? He took another step and looked back at Carla. "We're close," he said.

"Close," she said, "is what loses ball games and horse races. Something's wrong, Jay-jay."

"Can't be." Carefully he advanced to the lip of the creek channel, then jumped back as the dirt gave way beneath his feet.

Carla moved up beside him and pointed. In a hushed voice she said, "Look."

In the fading light he could distinguish a dark blocky shape. The 'dobe. It had to be. His hope soared and as quickly died. No hut ever built came equipped with caterpillar tractor treads. "Tank," he said. "They left a tank behind. Must've busted down."

"Tank?" Carla said. "What's that gismo up front?"

Breathlessly they approached. Sensing disaster, Jay-jay touched a cold metal flank, smelled grease and lubricating oil, gazed at the high bucket seat and gear levers. Close. So very close. But no cigar. The gismo up front was a bulldozer blade.

"No!" she wailed. "Oh no!"

Beyond the bulldozer a gash twenty feet wide stretched through the undergrowth, straight as a highway, lined on either side by mountains of raw earth, upended brush, and slaughtered trees. An avenue of destruction that began who knew where and ended here, incomplete. Another monument to Mars, god of war.

"Why?" Carla said. "Why did they hack out a road here?"

"That's no road," he said. "It's a firebreak. So no fire can jump the creek. They got this far and quit."

"This far? Do you know where that—that monster—" She snatched a clod and hurled it against the dozer— "where it's parked?"

"I know," he said sadly and gaped at the neat precise havoc the giant blade had left in its wake. Firebreaks stitched across this whole arid countryside, almost as common as fences. Were fences, fences against fire. An army of men could sift through all those unimaginable tons of displaced dirt like so many ants and find what? A few moldy bones? Bones as fragile as Aunt Hattie's best china cups? Fat chance. The bulldozer was parked just about where the old adobe hut had stood, on its pulverized remains.

"It's not fair!" Carla cried.

"Tell it to the Marines," he said. "Maybe that dozer jock works union hours. Be back Monday morning to finish the job."

"We still have a few hours left to look."

"In the dark? With a shovel?" He sighed and shook his head. Too bad for Zink and Dowser. For Dr. Chen and the People's Republic of China. For Smith and Jones and Taiwan. Too bad for almost anybody you'd care to mention.

"On TV once," Carla said, "I saw this anthropologist demonstrate how he works to find old bones and stuff. He dug a narrow little trench straight across the site and—" She looked up at Jay-jay in the gathering dusk. A teardrop trembled on her lashes. "Please, Jay-jay. At least let's try."

Halfheartedly he stepped to the edge of the firebreak and turned over a few shovelsful. The soil was soft, almost powdery, and, except for one pocket of loose rock, the digging went fast. Anything to please Carla, he told himself. He hadn't realized how much hope she'd pinned on this. And on him.

About halfway across the break his shovel clunked some solid object just below the surface. Another rock, he supposed, and bent down to pry it loose. Carla knelt beside him. His fingers closed over a piece of metal. He rubbed off the dirt and held it up, puzzled at first, and then recognized the thing: a broken padlock.

A large old-fashioned padlock, green with corrosion, deeply scratched and mashed thin, as if by some heavy weight. Like a ten-ton bulldozer. He could barely make out the four letters on the face: USMC.

"United States Marine Corps," Carla said. "Wasn't Peking Man smuggled out of China in military footlockers?"

"That's Moose Majeski's story anyway."

"So this padlock could be off the very same—"

"Could be," Jay-jay said. "But now we'll never know."

Carla's faith died hard. "Why not. If we—"

"Because," he said and touched her shoulder lightly, "if a dozer can squash a steel lock, think what would happen to a skeleton half a million years old."

She remained silent a long while, then stood up, and smiled too brightly. "I guess this wasn't in the cards for us," she said. "Or in the stars. I'll always wonder if we almost struck it rich."

He led her back through the brush out to the clearing's edge, ever vigilant for MPs. It was almost dark when they reached the culvert, crawled through under the fence, and started up the road toward home. Once he glanced back at the black winding course of Las Pulgas Creek and fingered the battered padlock in his pocket. Just a hunk of junk now. Busted hardware. Scrap.

They were almost at the farm before Carla spoke again. "Jay-jay," she said, "you haven't mentioned Creep all day."

"I've been thinking though," he admitted.

"So have I," she said. "And I have a theory."

He laughed. Carla was not a girl to stay depressed for long.

"Maybe it's funny to you," she said, "but listen. He's a wetback, an illegal alien, looking for a farm job at good wages in the US. Thousands sneak over the Mexican border every week. That's only fifty miles away."

"A Mexican wet?"

"He's hiding out from the Immigration fuzz. Border Patrol. He got this far and panicked. Everything fits."

"Everything but his clothes," Jay-jay said. "Creep doesn't wear any. Not even shoes. Zip."

"So come up with a better idea," she retorted.

Jay-jay smiled to himself in the darkness. He had a theory of his own but it would keep until he'd done some homework. No point in crossing swords with Carla at this late hour. It had been a long unnerving day.

All he had to show for it was a final worthless souvenir from Camp Hobart T. Pennington, that never-never land of surprises. And a few fond foolish memories.

By seven o'clock next morning Jay-jay was busy in the garden catching up on neglected chores. By eleven he'd finished the watering and by noon he was in town, having hitched a ride on a passing delivery van.

At the Ford agency he bought a new rotor for his pickup, to replace the one snatched by Smith and Jones. Then he entered the Hilldale Public Library.

With the aid of a librarian he located the section dealing with anthropology, a subject about which his ignorance was vast. Browsing through a book on local Indians, he learned that the first Americans had arrived in California at least twenty thousand years ago, after crossing a land bridge from the continent of Asia to Alaska and working their way south.

A long and hazardous journey, Jay-jay thought, and only the hardiest had survived. Some of their descendants still lived near here, scattered about on reservations. His Creep theory took a leapfrog jump.

To further satisfy his curiosity he next consulted a volume on Peking Man, that much earlier specimen of humanity, and studied the artist's conceptualized sketch. No beauty, to be sure: Peking Man had broad muscular shoulders, short legs, and long arms that dangled almost to his knees. His face had a receding chin, low forehead, a bony ridge above the eyes, and prominent cheekbones. "He looked," said the caption, "like a primitive version of the present-day Chinese."

Jay-jay scribbled some notes and read on.

Peking Man probably wore few clothes, mostly animal skins. He was a wanderer, a hunter of seeds and roots and wild fruits. He made stone tools. He probably had developed a simple form of speech. He used fire. He probably lived in a small group of several families that shared work and food. Probably, probably. A few facts and lots of guesswork.

Jay-jay closed the book and shut his eyes trying to imagine a day in the life of a Peking teen-ager. One not unlike that twentieth-century harvester of natural foods named Dowser. Most likely you went hungry half the time and ran scared always. Scared of wild animals and demons in the dark and hostile tribes invading your turf. Only a cave for shelter, or maybe a hut of sticks and leaves. For cover, a rabbit pelt G-string.

All in all, Jay-jay decided, he'd settle for the Flea Farm, USA, circa 1978.

When he reached home late that afternoon he found Aunt Hattie on her knees probing the soil in her experimental plot with a trowel. "How are your creets coming?" he asked.

"They're not," she said. "Too much fertilizer, I'm afraid."

"Well, they got a hundred-gallon dose," he reminded her. "Plus a lightning bolt."

Hattie sighed and then brightened. "I have a new idea, Jay-jay. An odorless garlic."

"Odorless?"

"Yes. The smell offends lots of people, you know. Bad breath. If I can cross garlic with mint—a garmint."

"A mint flavored garlic? Sounds real tasty." He gave her shoulder a pat. "Any calls for me today? Dr. Chen? Majeski?"

"No," she said, "but that real estate salesman phoned again."

"P. Martin Huff; Mister Azure Acres? What's he after now?"

"Never did find out. I held the receiver so and gave him the bird." Hattie stuck out her tongue and demonstrated. "Real loud. Then hung up."

Jay-jay grinned. "Some people just can't take a hint," he said.

After supper Hattie set out a glass and pitcher of water on the potting table in the backyard, then disappeared at the far end of the garden. Five minutes later she returned with a bowl of freshly picked late-season strawberries, which she placed beside the pitcher. "I can't seem to fetch him with my cookies," she explained. "Maybe these will tickle his fancy."

"You're leaving these berries for Creep?" Jay-Jay said. "Our best cash crop?"

"I have that poor boy on my conscience," Hattie said. "Don't suppose you'd like to sit up again tonight and watch for him?"

Jay-jay shook his head. "Can't hardly hold my eyes open."

Regarding the heavens thoughtfully, she said, "Jay-jay, all the signs are favorable. Whatever vittles our friend favors, something tells me he's a fool for strawberries."

"Carrots are cheaper," Jay-jay said. "But you could be right. G'night, Aunt Hattie."

He climbed to his room and made his nightly survey of the farm. The Santa Ana had gone, leaving as its visible scar the fire-blackened patch beside the creek. Over among the sycamores an owl hooted. An omen of things to come? Things like higher taxes? Bigger bills? Huff and his subdivision? It would be so easy to give up, sell out, move away. Easy, yes, but it would break Aunt Hattie's heart. He shook off his gloomy mood. "Creep," he said. "Are you listening out there, Creep? Please, no rocks tonight. Don't wake me up. I gotta recharge my batteries."

# THIRTEEN

BIG RED, THE rooster, sounded reveille as usual at sunup. Jay-jay hopped out of bed and dressed quickly. Outside his window the sky held promise of a pearly dawn, of a spanking brand-new day. Quiet reigned in the direction of Camp P. No sound of gunfire, no muted growl of heavy engines, tanks, or artillery. Or bulldozers. Apparently Operation Slasher was still on the shelf.

Tempted to sneak back for one last search, Jay-jay resisted. Peking Man was just a gleam in your beady little eye, he told himself; gone with a blink. On this fine fresh morning think positive, chum.

He headed for the kitchen but on impulse turned aside to check the table by the shed. The water pitcher and glass stood untouched. The bowl—he stepped closer and stared. The bowl, except for a pink stain of juice, was empty. Look, Ma, no strawberries! he thought in one giddy mind-bending flash. Not a berry left. Somebody had eaten them all.

Jay-jay peered all about the garden and saw nothing out of place, but once again he had that acute sense of being watched. Somebody—Creep—was spying on him. Whichever way he turned he could almost feel the impact of staring eyes. No imagination this time, no fluttery nerves. Creep had him in full view, he knew it. But from where?

He poured himself a glass of water and downed it in a gulp as cold perspiration beaded his forehead. Why the sweat? he asked himself. He wasn't afraid of Creep. He'd been angry at first, then puzzled, consumed with curiosity, but never afraid. Sure, Creep had filched a few vegetables. So what? In his own peculiar way Creep had tried to help. No guardian angel maybe, but as a trouble spotter, throwing rocks in the night. When you got right down to the nitty-gritty, Jay-jay realized he'd come to think of Creep as a friend, strange but sort of comforting to have around, even if you never saw him.

There were no footprints. But several yards beyond the table Jay-jay noticed a tiny sprig of green. He knelt and poked it with a twig. Leaves, a strawberry stem. Aunt Hattie, he recalled, hadn't hulled the berries last evening; she'd left them in their natural unwashed state. And why hadn't Creep discovered the berry patch before now? Probably because it was covered with a net to keep off thieving birds.

Another stem some distance beyond the first caught Jay-jay's eye. Then a third. And a fourth. Creep had walked this way along the garden path, gobbling berries and spitting out stems as he went, unaware of the leafy trail he'd left behind. It led straight to the base of the water tower.

Jay-jay pulled up short, thinking furiously. During the past week he'd searched the farm from end to end, not once but several times. He'd looked everywhere. Well *almost* everywhere. It had never occurred to him that Creep might be sharing his pad, so to speak. Living and sleeping cheek by jowl practically, buddy-buddy, all this while only a few feet away. Too obvious, or something.

'Fess up, Dowser. You're a slow learner. You're dumb, dumb, DUMB.

He pulled open the door to the storage room. A feeble light filtered in through one small window festooned with cobwebs. The air was close and stale, suggestive of times long past, of years gone by. Pieces of discarded furniture, shrouded in dust cloths, loomed in the shadows like swollen gray ghosts.

"Creep," he called softly. "Don't be afraid. It's me."

A startled mouse scurried across the floor. Then silence, thick, unbroken silence. He called again and waited in the doorway until his eyes adjusted to the dimness; then he stepped inside and stared about at what Hattie called her "heirlooms." A hat rack. A hand-crank phonograph. A butter churn. A lady's sidesaddle. Vanishing Americana.

We oughta open a museum, he thought, and charge admission. But the realization struck him that no one had entered this room recently. Not Aunt Hattie or himself. Nor Creep. The only occupant was a mouse and a few spiders.

So guess again.

He backed out and walked around to the far side of the tower, what he thought of as the rear. A crude ladder nailed to the siding—more of Grandpa Gribben's cockeyed carpentry—led from ground level up three stories to the top of the old redwood tank. Two rungs were missing; the runners looked as rickety as toothpicks. How long, Jay-jay

146 /

wondered, since he had last climbed that? Not for years. Not since he'd been a daredevil hare-brained kid.

And then his glance fell on another green sprig at the foot of the ladder. He squinted up at the defunct water tower and broke into a smile. So simple when you knew the answer. Simple for the simpletons.

Jay-jay pondered, then hurried to the berry patch and refilled the bowl with another batch of Aunt Hattie's finest. Returning to the tower, he began his perilous ascent, fortified by a prayer to whatever gods looked after crazies and mountain climbers. A minute later he crawled out on top, winded and sweaty, careful not to glance at the ground far below.

From this vantage point, above treetop level, he had an unobstructed view of the farm and the countryside for miles around in every direction. Which solved another mystery: Creep had found himself not only a hidey-hole in the sky but also a perfect lookout.

Jay-jay crouched on all fours, catching his breath, and eyed a square, hinged hatch cover that lay almost flush with the roof. Through it you could descend another ladder into the tank's black spooky void. He'd been down there only once, long ago, a childhood exploration for which he'd been soundly paddled and warned to keep away forevermore.

Slowly he raised the hatch and peered in. There were a few chinks of light where ancient planks had warped and sprung their seams, admitting some fresh air. The odor was ripe, somewhat like that of the boys' locker room at Hilldale High after a basketball game, but stronger, a concentrated human essence. He heard a faint creaking noise, saw a blur of movement. "Hello," he called. "You okay?"

No reply.

What did you expect? Jay-jay asked himself. The Gettysburg Address? This guy must be terrified. Remembering Carla's theory about Mexican wetbacks, he asked in halting tenth-grade Spanish, "*¿Habla usted Inglés?*" Do you speak English?

Silence.

"*¿De dónde es usted, amigo?*" Where do you come from, friend?

More silence.

Gradually Jay-jay's pupils adjusted to the semidarkness. Now he could make out a naked boy or small man sitting on the bottom of the tank, arms locked about his knees, staring up at him with bright narrowed eyes. No, not quite naked. A cloth was knotted about his waist and loins. A shirt, a makeshift breechclout.

Jay-jay grinned in sudden comprehension. "You swiped that out of my laundry bag. From my room. You're not Spanish. What's your name?"

Creep opened his mouth, seemed to struggle a second, and closed it.

"Your name?" Jay-jay repeated. This one-way conversation was going nowhere fast. He plucked a strawberry from the bowl and dropped it down into the tank.

Creep hesitated, eyes still fixed on Jay-jay, then unlocked his arms, reached for the berry, stuffed it into his mouth, and spat out the stem.

Progress? Jay-jay wondered. He dropped another berry, which went the way of the first. Trying a new tack, he put his finger to his chest and said distinctly, "Me Jay-jay," then pointed at Creep. "You—?"

Creep wiped his lips with the back of his hand.

Phooey, Jay-jay thought. This corny *Me Tarzan, you Jane* routine. But how to break the ice, to communicate? And suddenly Creep uttered his first sound. "Jay-jay," he said in a high squeaky voice.

Jay-jay laughed. "Right. You've got it! Now you—" He pointed again and waited for the next response. And waited. Patience, he told himself. Don't rush the kid. Maybe Creep forgot his name, if he ever had one. So now pick a name, any name. He cast about for inspiration. Anything from A to Z. From Z to A. Why not? "I'm going to call you," he announced, " 'Zuma.' Z-U-M-A. Say it—ZUMA."

"Zoo-*mah*." Creep's lips twisted in what could have been a smile and he jabbed a finger against his chest. "*Zoo*-mah."

"You catch on fast, Zuma," Jay-jay said, elated by this success. "Now we have that squared away let's get out of here."

"Zuma," repeated Zuma as though trying on his new name for size. "Jay-jay."

"We'll have you talking like a native in no time," Jay-jay said. Leaning through the hatch, he held out the bowl and motioned. "Up you go."

Whether Zuma understood or not, strawberries won the day. He stood up and moved cautiously to the foot of the ladder, into the slanting shaft of early light.

Given this first close look, Jay-jay swallowed. Zuma was muscular and short with black straggly hair that hung down his back. His head, which seemed large for his body, had a receding chin and a bony ridge above deep-set eyes. His age was impossible to guess. Where, oh where, Jay-jay thought, have I seen a face like that?

Yesterday. In that library book. The artist's sketch. Peking Man? Impossible! Ridiculous!

Zuma clambered up through the hatch onto the roof and squatted beside the bowl. Scooping out a handful of berries, he offered one to Jay-jay and crammed the rest into his mouth. His arms, Jay-jay observed, were unusually long, reaching almost to his knees, and his smell close up was gross. Chances were that Zuma hadn't washed himself in weeks. Or months. If ever.

Jay-jay clenched his teeth and braved Grandpa's ladder again, then watched Zuma swing down it as nimbly as a chimpanzee. With no hesitation Zuma trailed him around to the front of the tower and up to the sanctuary of his room. He had barely closed the door behind them when he heard Aunt Hattie's voice.

"Jay-jay," she called from the yard. "Hit the deck."

He motioned Zuma to keep low and stepped to the open window. "Reporting for duty ma'am," he said.

"The police," Hattie said. "They're here."

"Police?" Jay-jay had a gut wrenching vision of MPs from Camp P in uniform, complete with clubs and side arms, dragging him off in handcuffs. "What do they want?"

"You. What've you been up to now, boy?"

"I'll be right down," he said. Retreating from the window, he took Zuma by the arm, lifted the coverlet draped over his bed, and pointed to the space under the springs. "Shhh!" he whispered and pinched his lips, hoping this would convey the need for secrecy.

"Shhh," Zuma whispered back and grinned widely, the first real emotion he had shown. Delighted as a five-year-old at hide an' seek, he squirmed under the bed.

Jay-jay lowered the coverlet, glanced at his meager assortment of toilet articles, grabbed a can of deodorant, and sprayed the air liberally. That might cut the smell in case they searched his room. With a whispered "Hang in there, Zuma baby," he squared his shoulders and went forth to face the forces of law and order.

Aunt Hattie's "police" proved to be only one, Deputy Hoyle, who was pacing up and down beside his cruiser in the driveway. He favored Jay-jay with a tight little smile and said, "That was speedy. You must be an early riser."

"Yes, sir," Jay-jay said. "Did you catch the firebug yet?"

"I'm working on it," Hoyle said. "Funny thing happened Sunday. MPs on the base arrested two characters in a closed fire zone. Near here. The security officer notified me."

"Did they confess?" Jay-jay said hopefully.

The deputy shook his head. "Turns out they're Marines. Told some cock-and-bull story. But the point is, for Saturday night they have an airtight alibi. They couldn't have set your fire."

"Oh," Jay-jay said. Smith and Jones, Marines? Liars they were, a couple of hard-nosed chiselers, but secret agents for Taiwan? Somebody had his wires crossed. Another red-hot myth shot down in flames. But who did set the fire? "What happens to them now?"

"A reprimand. Maybe they'll draw some extra duty." Hoyle shrugged. "Which brings us back to Nature Boy. He showed up again last night."

Jay-jay felt his ears redden. "He did? Where?"

Eyeing him closely, Hoyle went on. "Down the road a piece. About three o'clock this watchdog sets up a ruckus that roused the family. The owner switched on his outside spots and saw a hippie run across the lawn. Stealing avocados, he found out later."

"Was the hippie naked?"

"Next thing to it. Had on some crazy jockstrap, the man said."

Jay-jay wet his lips. Zuma's jockstrap and my shirt. With my name stencilled on the tail. Hoo-boy!

"So we know this creep's still hanging around. Five'll get you fifty he's your firebug. Any suggestions, Jay-jay?"

"No, sir."

The deputy gave his holster belt a hitch and laid one finger alongside his nose. "You don't seem very concerned about all this," he said. "Right in your backyard."

"Oh, I'm real concerned," Jay-jay said, his understatement of the year. "Did you find any footprints?"

"No prints. But he ran this way. I'll nail him, never fear."

"Good luck," Jay-jay said insincerely. "He's in bad trouble, huh?"

"Depends on his record. Probably some judge will pack him off to a state hospital for the criminally insane and throw away the key." Hoyle eased into his cruiser and started the motor. "By the way, I noticed a water pitcher on the table in your garden. You expecting company so early?"

"Why—uh," Jay-jay floundered, "it's for the birds. They get thirsty in this hot weather."

"Bird drinker, eh? Don't believe I ever saw one use a glass." Hoyle gave him a hacksaw smile. "Wonders never cease, do they?" He waved a hand and drove off.

He knows I'm lying this trip, Jay-jay thought. Knows it

but not why. When he figures that out he'll be back with a search warrant. Then goodbye, Zuma. *Hospital for the criminally insane . . . throw away the key.* Not if I can stop it, mister.

Aunt Hattie was waiting at the kitchen door when he returned. "What happened to my bowl of berries?" she wanted to know.

"It's up there." Jay-jay pointed at the water tower. "On our roof."

"Heavens to Beulah, how—"

"Aunt Hattie, this may come as a shock—" He drew in a long breath. "Our friend is in my room. Under my bed. Hiding."

"Hiding from that policeman?"

"Among other people. We have to help him."

Hattie's look of concern gave way to a roguish smile. "Lovely. We need some excitement around here. Invite him down for breakfast, Jay-jay. I'll mix up some yogurt and wheat germ."

"Aunt Hattie, there's a problem," Jay-jay said. "He's not used to our—um, life style. And he can't talk much."

"Is he a mute?"

"No, you might call it a language gap. Look, I'm in a rush. Introduce him to you later."

Jay-jay hurried into the house, grabbed the phone and dialed. Carla answered on the seventh ring. She sounded sleepy and not overjoyed to hear his voice. "Don't faint dead away," he said, "but I have a surprise for you. Get over here quick."

She yawned in his ear. "Jay-jay, you're a dear and all that schmoo," she said. "But I don't think I can stand any more of your surprises."

"This one you can't afford to miss. And bring your camera."

He ran to his room, closed the door, and drew the window curtain on the side toward the road. Just in case Deputy Hoyle took a notion to double back. "Okay, Zuma," he said. "Come on out. Nobody here but us chickens."

There was no sound or movement.

"Zuma?"

Nothing.

Jay-jay reached out a hand, lifted the coverlet, and peered under the bed. Zuma, alias Creep, was gone, leaving only a faint musty aroma.

# FOURTEEN

JAY-JAY GAZED IN disbelief, then stared at his watch. He had left Zuma alone for less than half an hour, confident that Zuma would stay put. Nobody had kidnapped him; he'd taken off himself, probably frightened half to death. Which proved that Jay-jay still had much to learn about his shaggy new bunkmate.

He stepped to the west window and found the screen unhooked. That explained how. Zuma had hung by his hands from the sill and dropped to the ground, concealed from Aunt Hattie or Hoyle or anybody else who might be watching from the other side. No trick at all for the Strawberry Kid. Now for the where.

Moving his desk chair to the center of the room, Jay-jay stepped onto the seat and with his baseball bat tapped three times on the ceiling. Surely the sound would carry up through the flooring of the tank above. But if Zuma was hiding there, or if he heard, he did not respond.

Jay-jay thumped again, harder, and still again. Negative. Three times three, the magic number. But could Zuma count?

He descended to the yard, walked to the rear of the tower, scaled Grandpa Gribben's rotten old ladder for the second time that morning and shone his flashlight down the hatch. The tank was empty.

Back on the ground he searched for footprints and found none. Nor had Zuma left a handy trail of stems to follow. Maybe, Jay-jay thought, he's gone to the creek for a drink, or back to wherever he came from. That Zuma, he's part ghost and part eel. He's vanished as completely as if he'd never existed.

Carla came striding breathlessly along the driveway, camera case slung over one shoulder. "This had better be sensational," she greeted him. "On an empty stomach yet."

"Gone," he said. "Zuma ran away. We have to find him."

"Zuma? Who's Zuma?"

"The Creep," Jay-jay said. "That's what I call him. He's an Indian."

"An Indian? He can't be! How do you know?"

Hastily he explained how he'd discovered Zuma in the water tank. "I did some homework in the library," Jay-jay went on. "Seems there was this tiny tribe called Zumas, never rounded up by white men. They lived wild, real Stone Age stuff, in the mountains back of here. One by one they died, got killed off, until—"

"And your Creep is the last of the Zumas?" Carla said.

Jay-jay nodded. According to history, back in the 1920s an aged starving Indian had stumbled into a nearby ranch and collapsed. He recovered long enough to tell an interpreter his story, which was that he had existed alone for years like some hunted animal, probably the sole survivor of his people.

"1920s?" Carla said. "Half a century ago?"

"Suppose," Jay-jay said, "that he was wrong. That a couple of other Zumas were still alive. They had a baby. And *he* grew up. That's *our* Zuma."

Carla stared at him critically. "Dowser, what have you been eating lately? Peyote beans, or funny mushrooms?"

"Strawberries, nothing but strawberries, honest Injun." Jay-jay snapped his fingers. "Should've thought of that."

She followed him around the far side of the garden toward the brushy fringe of Las Pulgas Creek. At the berry patch, still shaded by a sycamore, he stopped and bent down. Loosening a tie, he raised one corner of the protective netting and then grinned. A pocket of moist dewy earth had been overturned and stripped of plants. Only minutes earlier.

"Smart little fellow," Jay-jay said. "He knew just where to find the place. Even covered his tracks."

"I can't believe this! I don't be—" Carla broke off with a gasp. "Eeeek!" she cried and stood stump still, open-mouthed and goggle-eyed.

Jay-jay glanced up and turned his head. Zuma had appeared from behind the tree as wraithlike as a wisp of smoke, his receding chin pink with juice, a sheepish look on his face. "Jay-jay," he said in his squeaky voice and pointed a finger at Carla. "Caa-lah."

She gave another gasp. "He knows my name!"

"Sure," Jay-jay said. "He's seen you here before, overheard us talking. I told you—Zuma's sharp as a razor."

Zuma, his eyes alight with curiosity, licked his lips and

scratched his navel. At the moment he seemed fearless. Maybe, Jay-jay speculated, Zuma had only been hungry. Was always hungry.

Carla recovered her aplomb quickly. "He's no Indian," she declared. "He's Asiatic. He looks like—like the Missing Link."

"That's not polite," Jay-jay said. "You'll hurt his feelings. Anyhow, all American Indians came from Asia originally. You can look it up."

"I will, believe me. And don't tell me he speaks English."

"Carla, just take his picture, will you. We can sort this out later."

She slipped her camera out of the case, made several adjustments, and peered through the viewer. "He's not very photogenic," she said.

Zuma watched her intently, puzzled now and slightly apprehensive. When the shutter clicked he flinched but held his ground. After several seconds Carla removed the print, waved it between thumb and forefinger, then handed it to Jay-jay, who passed it to Zuma. Zuma turned the photograph this way and that, held it close to his face, then at arm's length. His eyes grew wide. In a tone of wonder he said, "Zoo-mah," and giggled like a kindergartner.

"Bingo," Jay-jay said. "A winner. Now shoot him in profile."

Carla twisted a knob. "Darn!" she exclaimed. "That's the end of the roll. I'll have to get a new one from the house."

Together they studied the picture. Zuma looked like—well, nobody else but his own unique self. A face you couldn't forget or only a mother could love. Zuma would never be a teenybopper's heart throb.

The drone of an approaching car cut across the stillness. Jay-jay spun around, staring up the road, then frantically motioned Zuma to take cover. Unnecessary. Zuma already had melted from sight. One instant he'd been there, the next he was gone. Hocus-pocus, dominocus, alla-kazam! The Hindu rope trick—vanish into thin air.

The car went past without slowing.

"That Zuma," Carla said. "His eyes. The way he talks. I think he's Chinese."

"Chinese?" Jay-jay frowned. "Now who's on a crazy kick?"

"Jay-jay, what happened to those bones? Really happened?"

"What bones?"

"Don't play stupid." Carla's eyes bored into his. "That skeleton we found on Camp Pennington. You told me somebody stole it. You lied, didn't you?"

Jay-jay toed a clod of dirt and looked away. He wished he knew the secret formula, that he could fade out like Zuma. Face the music, chum, he told himself; you can't weasel out of this one. "Remember," he said, "how embarrassed you were when I found out about your father? Well, I have a skeleton in my family closet."

He told her how Aunt Hattie, unbeknownst to him, had ground the bones into meal and mixed it with liquid fertilizer, reminded her of the electro-culture experiment and the lightning bolt. The whole whacky schmear.

"Carla," he finished, "you know what some neighbors think of Hattie. If that story ever leaked out—I had to lie."

"Those toads. Your aunt's a darling." Carla nibbled

/ 159

her lower lip. "I wish you'd told me sooner. But of course! The bones got zapped!"

"Yup. And Hattie's creets. Electrocuted, I guess. Death by overdose."

" 'Perhaps death is life.' Some ancient Greek said that. Can you imagine—" A fierce exultant look flashed across Carla's face. "Now I know where Zuma came from!"

"So do I," Jay-jay said. "Agua Tibia, twenty miles from here. It's a government wilderness preserve."

"Never!" Carla cried. "Not on your life. And I can prove it!"

She hitched the camera over her shoulder, turned and ran.

He called after her but she hurried toward home, never pausing. Shaking his head, he stepped behind the sycamore to look for Zuma. That girl, he thought—she beats all. Zuma, a Chinese!

Zuma reappeared as dramatically as he had vanished, and as unpredictably. Suddenly he was there, emerging from the brush, a pleased, almost smug glint in his yellow eyes. What goes on inside his head? Jay-jay wondered. What's he feeling now? He seems to trust me some. But he's learned to be leery of cars.

"Good boy, Zuma," he said. "Now we're going to have a little quiz. Listen good because your neck—and maybe mine—depends on it."

Zuma uttered a sound somewhere between a cough and a grunt which Jay-jay translated as affirmative. Yes.

Jay-jay made a follow-me gesture and Zuma trailed along docilely into the creek bed among the boulders and undergrowth, to the edge of the burned-over patch. They crouched down, out of sight from the road or any chance passerby. Jay-jay crumbled a handful of charred rubble and said, "You won't understand at first but I'll go slow."

Zuma coughed again. Yes, Or was it?

"The law is after you, Zuma. They think you set this fire. You and I know better. But we have to prove somebody else did it. Do you know who? Did you see him?"

No comment.

Well, nobody said this would be easy, Jay-jay told himself. Are we on the same wave length? He pulled a booklet of matches from his pocket, struck one, and touched it to a dead leaf. The leaf burst into flame and he let it burn a moment, then snuffed it out. "Fire," he said. "Fire."

"Fi-yuh," Zuma repeated dutifully. "Fi-yuh."

Jay-jay heard another oncoming vehicle, waited until it rattled across the bridge. "Car," he said.

"Cah," Zuma duplicated.

Jay-jay nodded approval. Zuma had mastered two new words—*fire* and *car*. Teacher and student. Vocabulary. But the process was like wading through a pit of tar. And the next step would be even stickier. Could Zuma grasp an abstract concept?

Jay-jay pointed to himself. "Jay-jay, man," he said, then pointed at Zuma. "Zuma, man. Man, man, man."

Zuma coughed once again. Yes.

"Right," Jay-jay said. Three words now. His watch read eight o'clock. More traffic and people moving about. And always the specter of Deputy Hoyle snuffling around. "The way I figure," he said, "on Saturday night you came to the creek for a drink. You saw a car, a man, and the fire he lit. You ran back to the tower and woke me up."

No comment.

/ 161

With a twig Jay-jay scratched the outlines of three human figures in the dust, one large, one medium, one small—the sort of graphics for which he'd earned a C-minus in high school art—and touched the first. With his other hand he sketched three levels in the air. "Like so," he said. "Big man?"

Balanced on his heels as lightly as a tumbleweed, Zuma regarded Jay-jay with brilliant unblinking eyes, then turned his gaze downward to the creek bed and studied the figures. After a long silence he growled in his throat.

No? Negative? Could Zuma grok the relationship of measurements, of height and size?

Jay-jay touched the second shape.

Growl.

Jay-jay moved his finger to the third and last.

After some deliberation Zuma coughed.

Jay-jay sighed. A breakthrough? He could only hope. "So you saw a small man," he said. "How close?"

Zuma stared uncomprehendingly.

Idiot question, Jay-jay realized. Back to the drawing board. He went through another pantomine. First, length of hair. A bald man? Crew cut? Hat? No response. He finger-circled his eyes. Man in glasses? Blank. Nose? Ears? Zero.

But the next one—man with beard—triggered a reaction. Zuma gave an excited little bark and bared his teeth in a grin.

Encouraged, Jay-jay said, "The man had whiskers?" He tried to picture the scene through Zuma's eyes. Bright moonlight. Zuma, gifted with the night vision of an owl, must have witnessed the action from his "waterhole" a few

yards away. The torch, Mr. Firebug, X. "Now we're getting warm."

Stepping to the nearest oak, Zuma reached up and pulled out a strand of Spanish moss. He wadded it under his nose and clamped it in place with his upper lip, so that the ends drooped down over the corners of his mouth.

Jay-jay stared. The absurd clump plucked a chord of memory. Of what? Of whom? Then he had it. Fu Manchu, the Chinese mastermind of crime, the villain you loved to hate, with his sinister rattail—"Mustache!" Jay-jay cried. "No beard. Whimpy guy with a mustache. Yipes!"

Zuma tossed the moss into the air and giggled again.

Jay-jay considered. Not much of a description. Southern California swarmed with small mustachioed men. But it just might be the clincher if he got lucky. "See," he said and pointed to his eye. "Zuma see car?"

"Zuma see cah," said Zuma.

"What color car Zuma see?"

Sober attentive silence.

Maybe Zuma was color-blind. Anyway you sliced it, color was a complex idea to act out in charades. Jay-jay scrabbled in the creek bed and after a search found three pebbles, each a different hue. Holding out the first, he said, "Red."

"Yed," Zuma said.

"Zuma see *red* car?"

Growl. No.

Pebble number two. *Black* car?

No.

*White* car?

Long hesitation. No.

Another vehicle, invisible through the brush, whizzed over the bridge. Jay-jay mopped his face. He could feel the buildup of body heat down in these sweltering bottoms, the pressure of time. So much might hinge on these next few seconds. Now, for his star pupil, the final exam, the acid test. He fished a mint penny from his pocket and held it up to the sun. "Zuma see bronze car?"

Zuma took the coin, examined it, rubbed it between his palms, bit it, scraped it with his thumbnail. "See bonze cah," he said at last. Cough cough. Yes yes.

"Bull's-eye!" Jay laughed and clapped him on the back. Zuma and the goddess of gamblers had come through like champions. Zuma had given him not legal evidence perhaps, but the one hard fact he needed.

Grinning hugely, Zuma made chewing motions with his mouth and patted his belly.

"Hungry?" Jay-jay said. "So am I. Zuma, you just earned yourself a bonus. Come on."

They climbed out of the bottoms and, weaving through the brush, Jay-jay led the way back to the sycamore tree. He signaled Zuma to keep down, stepped out into the garden, folded back the bird net, and surveyed the depleted strawberry patch. Slim pickings. But he gathered up every ripe berry in his bandanna and retreated. Hunkered down behind a boulder, he and Zuma polished off the last of Aunt Hattie's top-dollar crop in companionable silence.

For the moment Jay-jay's tensions unwound. No sweat. No hassles. Fun in the sun. But it couldn't last, he realized, this false sense of security. Zuma would never be safe here unless some mammoth miracle came to pass. How could he warn Zuma of his danger? Or should he?

Maybe Zuma knew. "School's out," he said. "Time to go to work."

Emerging from the undergrowth behind the water tower, Jay-jay peered across the yard and out to the road. All clear. With his fingers and some body English he gave Zuma an order. Up. Stay there till I signal you down.

Zuma coughed. Yes. With glee in his eyes.

"Zuma—" The occasion called for something more, Jay-jay felt obscurely. A gesture. A symbol. How long since he'd first met Zuma face to face? Not four hours ago. He thrust out his right hand, gripped Zuma's limp one, and squeezed. "Shake," he said. "Friend."

Surprised, Zuma withdrew his hand, looked at it, then looked into Jay-jay's face. "Fend," he said in his high-pitched voice. *Friend.* Zuma had acquired one more word.

With a bound he mounted the ladder like an Olympic gymnast and disappeared over the roof.

# FIFTEEN

JAY-JAY PARKED his pickup in front of the Zink house and sat for a moment listening to Daddy's "typewriter." Carla was one gutsy gal, no doubt about it. Independent, stubborn, obstinate as a mule. But with soul. As for Daddy, the absentee author, refugee from alimony payments, he figured somewhere in this dilemma.

Daddy would be heard from, Jay-jay felt sure. If not in person, then in spirit.

He crossed the lawn and knocked. Carla opened the door on its chain and peeked out, then let him into the cluttered living room and shut off the tape. "I hoped you might be Daddy," she said. "He's been gone so long."

"Sorry to disappoint you," Jay-jay said, noting a pile of brightly jacketed books on the corner desk. "Did he write all those?"

"Those and dozens more," she said. "I'm doing some homework of my own. On Zuma. I still can't believe he's real."

"He is. He told me who set the fire." Jay-jay handed her a card on which he'd written a name and telephone number and some instructions.

Carla read it and frowned. "Never heard of him."

"Lucky you. But he's real too. I need help, Carla. First, can I borrow your tape recorder for a few hours?"

"Not unless I know why."

"You don't want to know. Next, ring this number. You'll probably get his secretary. Tell her you're The Elemental Seed. That's a food co-op in town, my home away from home. Read this message: 'Dowser is ready to deal.' Got it?"

"That's all? 'Dowser is ready to deal.' "

"Yup. Five little words. Then give her the time and place and hang up. Your good deed for today."

Carla tapped the card against her teeth and regarded him with her steady clear-eyed gaze. "Anonymous phone call? Secret rendezvous. Who're you working for now, the CIA?"

"Will you do it?"

"Jay-jay, did I ever tell you I'm a scaredy-cat? A coward? Also I happen to have a few principles. Why should I stick my neck out for you like that?"

"Not for me," he said. "For Aunt Hattie."

"Is this her idea?" Carla said.

"Mine," Jay-jay said. "She doesn't know a thing about it. Any reward you get will be in heaven."

"Whose heaven?" Carla's eyes softened. "I'm not much into her astrology thing but—for Aunt Hattie I guess I can stretch my scruples a mite. Just so it doesn't become a habit." She sat down at the desk and pulled the telephone toward her. "Now?"

"Now."

She dialed, spoke into the mouthpiece in a calm even voice, waited several seconds, then delivered the message twice. Replacing the receiver, she looked up at Jay-jay with a Mona Lisa smile. "How'd I do, professor? Fluff my lines?"

"Perfect," he said. "An Oscar performance."

"The secretary put me through direct," Carla said. "He didn't sound suspicious, but what if he smells a rat?"

"What I hope he smells," Jay-jay said, "is lots of crisp fresh cash. Like a bee homing in on honey."

"Bees sting, you know. Killer bees."

Jay-jay shook his head in mock reproof. "There you go again, spreading joy and cheer. Relax. This bee doesn't even buzz."

"That's the deadliest kind," Carla said. "They sneak up on your blind side, then ZING! I'm going with you."

She started to rise but he put his hands on her shoulders and gently pushed her down in the chair. "Un-unh. I want you here for backup."

"Backup? What's that?"

"If I'm not back by four o'clock, call the sheriff's office. Ask for Deputy Hoyle."

"Why not call him now? Yourself. Arresting crooks is what he's paid for."

"What cop would buy Zuma's story?" Jay-jay asked. "In sign language? Not Hoyle. Hoyle's itching to toss Zuma in the slammer. I have to get some evidence first." He unplugged the recorder from the wall socket. "How are the batteries?"

"New this week." Carla opened a drawer and pulled out a plastic cartridge. "Here's a fresh tape."

"Won't need it," he said. "Any last minute advice?"

"None you'd listen to." Carla lowered her eyes and added in a scratchy voice, "Just be—oh, get out of here, you dope!"

Jay-jay carried the recorder to the truck and got in. He had two hours until his "appointment" but he wasted no time in driving up the hill past the farthest house and turning off onto the secondary road. The last occasion he'd come this way had ended in a painful lesson at the hands of Smith and Jones. To those two thugs, plus an assist from W. Zink, he owed the inspiration for this latest brainstorm, such as it was.

Live and learn, old buddy, he told himself. Fight fire with fire.

The road was as narrow and bumpy as he remembered it, and as deserted. It did not attract city drivers and freeway speed merchants. For his purposes it promised solitude and a few weekday hours of uninterrupted privacy. He could ask no more.

The truck labored up the final grade to the dead-end turnaround at Granada Reservoir. Jay-jay backed and filled, parked with the nose pointed downhill, ready for a quick getaway. Silence closed around him. He glared at the mangy eucalyptus trees, the gigantic boulders, the crumbling dam, the powder magazine. He wasn't likely to forget this place ever, not one detail.

Thanks a heap, Smith and Jones, he thought. I'll do as much for you someday.

He walked to the shed some fifty yards away and inspected the solid concrete walls. Escape proof as a bank vault, it had a half-inch slit under the door. With a pocket oil can he lubricated the hinges and bolt and swung the door back and forth several times to get the feel. The room itself, low ceilinged, an eight-by-eight cell, was black and foul. A cell without bars, solitary confinement.

He set Zink's recorder in the middle of the iron-hard earthen floor, depressed the tab marked PLAY, and turned the volume knob up to full. Then he backed out and left the door wide open.

Returning to the truck, Jay-jay busied himself with pen and tablet composing a statement. It was a laborious process. He scratched out words and whole sentences, crumpled page after page. At length he completed the task to his satisfaction, copied out a final draft, and tucked it back in the tablet.

From the cloudless sky the midday sun beat down, but a cooling breeze stirred off the Pacific. High noon. Unlike that other noon when he had waited here with a blistering Santa Ana at his back, an innocent in Toyland. This time he'd come to play, as the sportscasters said. A game with no rules or referees or overtime.

Eucalyptus leaves rustled like ghostly sandpaper. Overhead a red-tailed hawk dipped and planed. In the distance land and sea merged in a blurred horizon. Jay-jay stared down the mountainside. Would his man come, and if he did, alone? Or with escort?

So now you're a shrink, Dowser, he told himself. You have the patient on your office couch, reading his psyche. For a city slicker this man is naive. Downright gullible. An upward-and-onward achiever with an ego as big as the *Queen Mary*. But what if you read him wrong?

Far down the road a haze of cinnamon-colored dust appeared. Jay-jay heard the distant whine of an engine. He was leaning against a fender in a casual pose when, several minutes later, a bronze Mercedes rolled over the rise and braked to a stop, radio blaring.

P. Martin Huff, alone behind the wheel, dabbed his mustache with a handkerchief and wiped the dust off his hands. His eyes darted this way and that over the dam site. "Well, Jay-jay," he said, "so you finally saw the light at the end of the tunnel. Been waiting long?"

"Just got here," Jay-jay said. "How are you, Mr. Huff?"

"Frankly, I'm upset," the realtor said. "Had to cancel two appointments. Why couldn't we get together in my office instead of this godforsaken hole? Why the cloak-and-dagger bit?"

Staring in the window, Jay-jay saw a CB unit mounted on the panel. Instant communication. Which in part explained Huff's complacency. He had a huge backup audience out there. "Truth is, Mr. Huff, you know how Aunt Hattie feels about selling her farm. If she got wind of me meeting you—"

"You have a point," Huff conceded. He made another hasty survey of the reservoir, as though Hattie might be lurking somewhere in ambush, then killed his motor and radio and slid out of the car. He shot an elegant gold-linked cuff. "I'm due back in thirty minutes. Make this short and sweet."

Jay-jay put on his best country bumpkin face, wondering if the man was hard of hearing. "Gee, Mr. Huff, I don't rightly know where to start."

Huff made a grimace that might have been a polite sneer. "Why not start with money."

"The bonus you offered me the other day? The new car and the job?"

"Did I say that? Don't price yourself out of the market, sonny. I'll get that property eventually, on my terms." The realtor broke off abruptly and held up a hand. "What's that noise?"

Deadpan, Jay-jay said, "What noise?"

"Over there. Don't you hear it?"

Jay-jay cupped a hand behind his ear. "Sounds like a woodpecker."

Huff's eyeballs swiveled like a pair of gimbals. "There. In the bunker. It—it's a typewriter!"

"Doggone," Jay-jay said. "I'd've sworn nobody was around for miles."

Huff took two steps and stopped. "You!" he shouted. "In the shed!"

"Maybe some crazy writer getting away from it all," Jay-jay volunteered.

"Writer?" Huff wasted Jay-jay with a laser glance. "How'd he get here? Fly?"

"Somebody could've dropped him off," Jay-jay said. "My neighbor's like that. Writes books. Do anything for peace and quiet."

Ignoring him, Huff stepped closer to the shed and yelled again.

The rat-a-tat-tat of Daddy's "typewriter" went merrily on.

"Sure types up a storm," Jay-jay said. "Must be hitting sixty words a minute."

Huff advanced still nearer and halted, his face redder by the second. "Dowser, if this is one of your aunt's tomfool stunts—"

"Shucks, she's not that batty. Anyway, she can't type a lick. Wonder who it is, Mr. Huff."

The realtor hesitated, torn between suspicion and curiosity.

"Maybe," Jay-jay said, "you want to call the whole deal off."

Curiosity won. Lured like a snake to a charmer's irresistible flute, Huff edged toward the open doorway and paused on the threshold. He drew a gold cigarette lighter from his pocket, held it aloft, and peered inside.

Half a step behind him, Jay-jay said, "Anybody you know?"

Suddenly aware of his peril, the realtor tried to retreat.

Jay-jay planted a palm between his shoulder blades and shoved. Then he slammed the door shut and shot home the bolt. After a moment of silence he heard a tirade of obscenities, followed by a splintering crunch. That would be Daddy's recorder, smashed to smithereens. P. Martin Huff, Mr. Azure Acres, sounded unhappy.

Very quietly Jay-jay walked back to the turnaround, raised the hood of the Mercedes, removed the rotor, chucked it out into the brush, and disarmed the CB. Then he sat down in the shade and ate a leisurely brown-bag lunch. Entertained by the aerial antics of two swallows, he waited until all sound from the shed subsided.

With his tablet under one arm he approached the door once more, lay down on his belly, and placed his mouth to the crack. "Mr. Huff, can you hear me?"

Mr. Huff could. He roared and ranted and kicked the door and threatened Jay-jay with dire consequences.

Jay-jay heard him out, then said patiently, "You're getting hoarse, Mr. Huff. Why don't you lie down on the other side so you won't have to holler."

Mr. Huff hollered.

Jay-jay stood up, walked over to the reservoir, and practiced throwing rocks at a beer can for twenty minutes. When he returned, the shed was quiet. "Ready to talk now?" he said.

No answer but heavy breathing inches away.

"That's better," Jay-jay said. Evidently Huff had taken his advice about the prone position. Now they were almost nose to nose, eyeball to eyeball, separated by only a sheet of steel. "Or I can come back tomorrow."

"Dowser, you dirty rotten bleep! When I get out of here I'll sling your ass in jail so fast—"

"Temper, temper," Jay-jay said. "Why'd you set the fire? Figured to burn Aunt Hattie off her land? Was that your idea?"

Deep silence. Then the realtor said, "Fire? What fire?"

"I have a witness who saw you light it. Identified you right down to your mustache." Jay-jay grinned at the mental picture of Zuma on the witness stand, a wad of moss under his nose. "He'll talk, if you don't."

Another long silence. "You're bluffing. What's his name?"

"Don't tempt me, Mr. Huff. You could get awful lonely in there."

"What is it you want, Dowser? Money?"

"What I want," Jay-jay said, "is you off my back. What you want is out. Do we have a deal?"

"I'm listening."

"There's a paper in this tablet," Jay-jay said. "I'm going to shove it under the door. Read it. Use that fancy lighter. Sign it. Date it. Then shove it back and you're home free."

"I won't sign anything, you punk. That's blackmail!"

"So long, Mr. Huff."

"Dowser, wait—"

Jay-jay rose to his feet, walked to the truck, switched on the ignition, and revved up the motor. He left it running, walked back to the shed and dropped to his knees. "Last call, Mr. Huff," he said.

"Dowser, I can't. I won't!" The voice of P. Martin Huff seemed to have undergone a change. It had a whiney note, almost craven. "The publicity could ruin me."

"I hate to tell you this," Jay-jay said, not unkindly, "but a couple of hours from now, unless I head him off, a deputy sheriff named Hoyle will be up here with fire in his eye. That's a lousy pun. If you'd rather talk to him—"

Five minutes later Jay-jay picked up his tablet from the ground and carefully read Huff's signed statement. As a confession it might not hold up in court, or anywhere else, but as an insurance policy it would serve. A club to keep the realtor at bay, away from Hattie's farm. For a while. In this imperfect world, he told himself, you settle for the possible.

He yanked back the door bolt, turned and sprinted to his truck. Highballing down the hill, he exploded into laughter, the release of pentup stress. "Zuma, baby," he said aloud, "what are old friends for?"

# SIXTEEN

CARLA RAN OUT when Jay-jay drove up in front of the house. Her color high, eyes shining, she cried, "Are you all right? What happened?"

Feeling like a gladiator back from the arena with a victor's wreath on his brow, he said, "The good guys won."

"But that Huff, the firebug?" she said. "Isn't he in trouble?"

"Enough to keep him honest. For now. Till next time." Jay-jay was conscious of the silence, the absence of typewriter music. "We had one casualty. Your recorder. It got stomped."

"Never mind, I won't need it now," Carla said. "Daddy's coming home tonight. He just phoned."

"Great. I hope he stays a while."

"So do I. But, Jay-jay—"

His euphoria faded. He sensed from her voice, from her air of suppressed excitement, that Carla had not yet told him all. And for some obscure reason he wasn't sure he wanted to hear any more on any subject from Walter Zink's daughter, soul or no soul, not at this moment.

"Jay-jay, brace yourself for a shockeroo."

He followed her into the living room, which appeared even more disorderly than when he'd left it. Books lay scattered on the floor, open and face down, as though Carla had gone on a frantic reading binge.

"Excuse the mess," she said. "It took me hours to lay hands on the right one. Do you know what a 'clone' is?"

"Clone? First cousin to a clown?"

She thumbed open a dictionary. "Here's a definition, from the Greek word for 'twig': 'All the descendants derived from a single individual, as by cuttings or bulbs; or by fission.' "

"You mean breeding new kinds of plants?" he asked. "Hybrids? Like Hattie's creets?"

"Not exactly, but you're on the right track." Carla ran her finger down the column. "Here's more: 'Cloning, the technique of producing a genetically identical duplicate of an organism; mononuclear reproduction.' "

"Well, that's very interesting but—"

"And not only plants," she said. "Animals too. And humans. Zuma is no Indian. He's a clone."

Jay-jay stared, uncertain whether to laugh or reason with her or pat her on the head.

Carla snatched a book off the couch and opened it to a marker. "This is one of Daddy's early novels, about biological research in outer space. The leader is explaining to some earthlings: 'Here on Planet Qworg we have developed cloning to a high art. By sophisticated application of electro-synthesis we can reenergize individual cells, or complete organisms that have been dead for centuries.' "

"I hope the earthlings understood," Jay-jay said. "I sure don't."

Carla read on: " 'If we had a toenail clipping or a bone from the remains of, for example, William Shakespeare, who died in 1616, we could re-create a new Shakespeare. Who perhaps would write another *Hamlet*. What a boon to the universe that would be.' "

"All I can say," Jay-jay said, "is your father has some imagination. Bring a dead man back to life? That's strictly Frankenstein."

"Not so," Carla said. "It's happened here, on earth, more than once. In research labs. With rats and frogs. So why not people?" She laid down the book and faced him squarely. "You're afraid to admit it, Jay-jay."

"But Aunt Hattie—"

"She's always experimenting with genes. Plant genes. But this time she added something new. Human cells. Fertilizer. Not just a toenail cutting or one bone. A whole skeleton."

Jay-jay was beginning to feel a little woozy. Dear, sweet old Hattie, a monster maker?

"Step two, the thunder storm," Carla went on relentlessly. "Electro-culture. The lightning bolt. Synthesis. Fission. What Hattie created, by accident, was a copy of Peking Man. Or Peking Boy. A clone five-hundred-thousand-years old!"

Accident? Jay-jay thought. Dear God, what have I got up in the water tower?

"I told you this would blow your mind," Carla said. "Mine too. Wipeout. Until I got thinking what this means to science. Zuma, sensation of the century. He's worth a fortune!"

"Fortune?" Jay-jay echoed weakly. "What do we do— haul him around in a cage like a circus freak?"

"Of course not. I don't have money on the brain, dollar signs in my eyes, like some types I could mention. Zuma doesn't belong to us, he belongs to all the people. To the world. Think big, Jay-jay."

"Nobody's asked Zuma what *he* thinks."

"Let's wait till Daddy gets here. He'll know what to do. After all, he wrote the book."

"But Zuma's not in a book. He's not in outer space. He's here, on the farm. Now. He gets hungry and thirsty and scared, just like you and I do. He's a person. And we've got to protect him."

"Too late," she said. "He's been seen. The fuzz are after him. They don't know *what* he is, yet—"

"He's an Indian!" Jay-jay shouted.

"That's what you say. But he'll be the Eighth Wonder of the world. You can't keep this hushed up. A week from now, or sooner, a zillion gawkers will be camped on your doorstep like vultures. Slobbering for meat."

Jay-jay shuddered. Carla was right about that part. The nurse, the avocado grower down the road, Deputy Sheriff Hoyle. One of them would talk. The story would spread like brush fire. In his mind he saw lurid newspaper headlines: MONKEY MAN. HILLDALE MONSTER. MYSTERY BEAST. NAKED CREATURE STALKS BY NIGHT.

"Go home quick and watch him close," she said. "I'll ring you the minute Daddy gets here."

In a fog of confusion Jay-jay found his way out to the truck. Right? Wrong? Mister-in-Between? He had no answer. No solution. He had finally arrived at the last drop-off. The crunch. With nowhere to go.

As he turned into the farm a dark sedan swung off the road and pulled up behind him. A bear of a man in a chauffeur's cap slid from behind the wheel and opened a rear door. Dr. Chen, the cultural attaché from Peking, stepped down.

"Hello, doctor," Jay-jay said. "You're just in time for tea."

"Unfortunately I cannot partake of your hospitality on this occasion," said Dr. Chen in his grave courtly way. "I am returning to my homeland in a few hours."

"Back to China?" Jay-jay said.

"That is the case. To report the failure of my mission here. A great disappointment."

Jay-jay glanced at the bodyguard, then back at Chen. In his thick horn-rimmed glasses the doctor looked like a mournful owl.

"This morning," Chen went on, "as a last resort I interviewed those two individuals, Smith and Jones. Under detention in the brig. Most uncooperative. They referred me to you. In somewhat coarse language. I might add."

Jay-jay discovered he still could grin. "My pals. By now every Marine on the base must know about your bones."

"Too true, I fear." Chen sighed and regarded Jay-jay reflectively. "So, Mr. Dowser, have you any final information to impart?"

Jay-jay risked a glance at the water tank and as quickly looked away. He had no grievance against Dr. Chen. In fact he felt sorry for the man. Who else had ever offered him half a million dollars, or would again? A dollar for every year of Peking Man. "Dr. Chen," he said, "there *were* some bones—"

After Jay-jay finished his account about the 'dobe hut

beside Las Pulgas Creek, Operation Slasher, the firebreak, the bulldozer, Dr. Chen remained silent for a long while, studying the tips of his shoes. When he did look up his eyes were moist. He coughed into his handkerchief and cleared his throat and said in a sad thin voice, "Destroyed by bulldozer. How barbarian. And nothing escaped?"

"One busted padlock." As a gesture of consolation Jay-jay added, "But maybe those weren't the Peking bones. They could've belonged to anybody."

"Possibly. I thank you for your frankness."

Chen turned toward his limousine, a picture of dejection, and Jay-jay took pity. But more than that, much more, he could not bear not to hear a verdict from the lips of a man who might be the world's foremost expert. From his shirt pocket Jay-jay pulled out the picture of Zuma that Carla had snapped with her instant camera. "What do you think of this?"

As Chen examined the photograph a strange expression crept over his face. "Very lifelike," he said. "Where—"

"A friend took it," Jay-jay said. "In a—a museum. Exhibit in a showcase."

"Indeed. What museum?"

"She didn't say. A bug on anthropology but kind of spaced out." Jay-jay flicked another look at the water tank. Was Zuma watching? If so, what would he make of it? "Dr. Chen, does it look like the real Peking Man would've looked, way back when?"

"Exactly. Every detail. Amazing. It's so realistic that I—" Chen seemed lost in reverie, a frown stitched across his forehead. And then, surprisingly, he smiled. "Except for the loin cloth. That has an, ah, contemporary look."

Wisely, Jay-jay said nothing. A sensation like prickly heat began to spread over his entire body.

"I would like," Chen continued, "to make a very special request. May I keep this?"

Jay-jay hesitated. Why not? He owed the doctor something. One picture was little enough. A memento. He, Jay-jay, could shoot all he wanted, any time. "Sure," he said. "Compliments of the house."

"I am in your debt. We Chinese have a ceremonial toast: *Shou lu*. 'Long life and happiness,' it translates." Dr. Chen signaled to his bodyguard and stepped back into his car with the silken composure of a Ming Dynasty mandarin mounting his sedan chair. "Farewell, Mr. Dowser. But as one of your famous generals once said, 'I shall return.' "

Jay-jay waited until the doctor had disappeared down the road, then he ran to the tower. Once in his room, the door closed, he climbed up on a chair and tapped the ceiling three times with his bat. "All clear, Zuma," he called. "You can come down now."

Zuma didn't answer.

Jay-jay raised his voice. "Zuma, hey, wake up!"

Silence.

Only then did Jay-jay notice the object on his desk, a faded blue work shirt. He held it up and read his name stencilled on the tail. Zuma's borrowed loincloth, his make-do G-string. Zuma had returned it to its source, unlaundered but intact.

Jay-jay crossed to the window and poked his head out. He looked first toward the strawberry patch, then craned his neck and peered up at the tank. Slowly comprehension came, like water percolating sand. No need to climb that ladder again, or search behind the sycamore. Zuma was gone, the shirt his goodbye. It was as final as a handshake, the last hurrah. Enter naked, exit naked, a whole life cycle.

Jay-jay struggled to readjust his thoughts. Why? he wondered. Was it because Zuma had sensed that what passed for civilization was closing in like a net? Did Zuma know, in the core of his being, that he "belonged" to no one but himself? Indian or clone or whatever, he was an alien in the twentieth century, stranger in a hostile land, prisoner in a water tank. And so he'd fled.

Where? Well, that depended on your point of view, Jay-jay decided. Personally, he favored the government wilderness preserve at Agua Tibia. Lukewarm Water. Hot springs. At least Zuma could take a bath. As for any other place—

Dr. Chen, the seeker of Peking Man, might return someday. But would Zuma? Maybe next strawberry season.

"Yoo-hoo, Jay-jay!" Aunt Hattie called from the yard. "Telephone."

He groaned. That would be Walter Zink, science-fictioneer and matrimonial dodger, the typist who wasn't there. Daddy and his earthlings and Qworg planets and mad biologists. With Carla he could cope, just barely, but with Daddy?

"It's the nice boy in the yellow T-shirt," Hattie yelled.

"Who?"

"The Leo, the big one. Heavens to Bridey, don't you remember?"

Jay-jay descended from his room, hurried to the house, and grabbed the phone.

"Hi ya, kiddo," a familiar gravel voice assaulted his ear. "How's business?"

Jay-jay grinned. Did absence make the heart grow fonder? Despite everything, he'd missed that voice and the sergeant who went with it. "Not so hot, Moose," he said. "What's new?"

Moose Majeski minced no words. "Have a proposition for you," he growled. "Operation Slasher is off. Kaput. Operation Survival is back on. Get the picture?"

"Sort of," Jay-jay said warily. "When?"

"Tomorrow night. Same time, same place. Ten starvin' lard-butt Gyrenes. With cash."

"Look, Moose, I can't—"

"A hundred bucks for you," the sergeant said. "Some small change for me. And a present for Aunt Hattie if she bakes an extra batch of cookies."

"Moose, isn't it against the law?"

"What law says a hungry man can't eat? It's a living, kiddo. Have we got a deal?"

Jay-jay rubbed his forehead. *It's a living.* Sure, and we're brothers under the skin, you and me. A couple of wheeler-dealers. I'll probably end up in the Marines myself. Dat ole debil money. But somebody has to earn the bread to pay the taxes and keep Aunt Hattie in exotic plants. "Deal," he said. "See you at the fence some night, old buddy."

"Not me, you won't. Nor under it." Moose chuckled. "And tell that skinny gal of yours she ties one mean knot."

Jay-jay hung up and stared out the window, smiling, his conscience clear. Or almost clear. A vagrant breeze off the Pacific stirred Aunt Hattie's frayed lace curtains. Across the road, beyond the hills, the mountains rose in ridge upon unspoiled ridge, smoky blue against the sky. No Azure Acres yet. Was Zuma out there somewhere now, seeking a refuge of his own, living off the land? Like a Marine on survival training?

"*Shou lu.*" He repeated the Chinese toast under his breath. "*Shou lu*, Zuma. Long life and happiness."

HAL G. EVARTS, called by *English Journal* a "master of mystery," is well known as the author of many fast-paced novels for young readers. From childhood he wanted to be a writer, as was his father, and at an early age he began to accompany his father on his travels around the world. Mr. Evarts' career as a writer began in high school as a journalist on the school's newspaper and continued to flourish as the editor of Stanford University's Literary Yearbook. He has since written for magazines, newspapers, television, and the screen as well as producing over twenty novels. Mr. Evarts lives with his wife in La Jolla, California.